The Hunting of the Last Dragon

Also by Sherryl Jordan

Secret Sacrament

✠
✠

The Hunting of the Last Dragon

SHERRYL JORDAN

HARPERCOLLINSPUBLISHERS

For Kym, who has fought dragons and won,
and for little Kael, who may one day fight dragons of his own.
I wish you strength, and the knowledge that you are never alone.

Library of Congress Cataloging-in-Publication Data
Jordan, Sherryl.
The hunting of the last dragon / Sherryl Jordan.
p.   cm.
Summary: In England in 1356, as a monk records his every word, a young
peasant tells of his journey with a young Chinese noblewoman to St. Alfric's
Cove and the lair of a dragon.
ISBN 0-06-028902-3 — ISBN 0-06-028903-1 (lib. bdg.)
[1. Dragons—Fiction.   2. Chinese—England—Fiction.   3. Footbinding—
Fiction.   4. Middle Ages—Fiction.   5. Monks—Fiction.   6. Great Britain—
History—Edward III, 1327–1377—Fiction.]   I. Title.
PZ7.J7684 Hu   2002   2001039375
[Fic]—dc21   CIP
                                                                                AC

Map and interior drawings by Sherryl Jordan
Typography by Larissa Lawrynenko
1   2   3   4   5   6   7   8   9   10
❖
First Edition

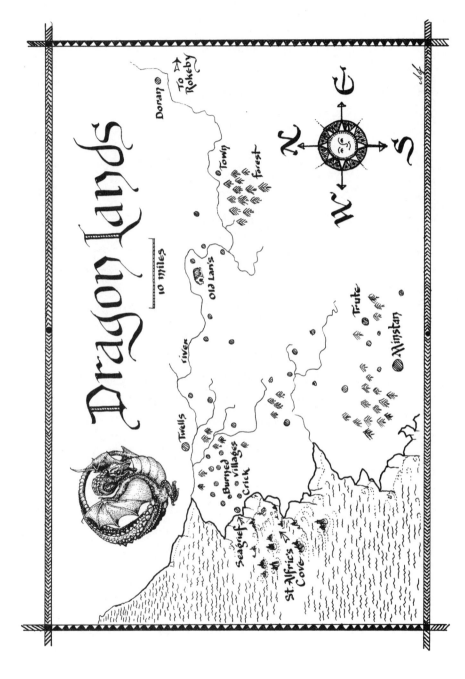

The Tale of Jude of Doran

As told to
Brother Benedict
at the Monastery of St. Edmund at Minstan,
who recorded it faithfully,
making this a true and correct record
of the hunting of the last dragon,
and of the events that happened
at St. Alfric's Cove

ONE

EAR IS SOMETHING I am well acquainted with. When I was a child I was afraid of nightmares and the dark, of bogeymen and fiends; more lately I've been afraid of being a failure or a fool, afraid of enemies, wolves, and hell, and of a witch who held, for a time, power over me; but none of these terrors equalled the fear I knew that day I first stood upon the ashen shore of St. Alfric's Cove, hardly able to breathe for the stench of dragon-fire and death, and certain to my bones that here, in this burned and bitter place, I would lose my life. And not mine only, but the life of my friend, Jing-wei.

If she knew any fear that awful day, Jing-wei did not show it. A long time she looked upon the scorched cliffs, up to the lofty cave where dwelled our deadly enemy. The stone immediately below the lair was black with soot or blood, and a corpse—I could not tell, for distance, whether it was man or beast—hung partly over the ledge. Another corpse lay on the beach not far from us, and that was a man, though I tried hard not to look at it. He was mainly bones burned to ash, and the remains of his hand still held his sword.

"We'll not fail, Jude," said Jing-wei, coming over to me, limping badly on the darkened stones. Her bandaged feet were black with soot, and grey ash-dust lay across her smooth lips and strange brown skin. She was all strange—small, and impossibly delicate considering the task ahead of her. "We'll not fail," she said again, taking my arm and turning me away so I could not see the burned soldier. She did not speak again for a while, but only looked up that savage cliff, her almond-shaped eyes as black as coal and full of secrets too deep for me to read. So still she stood, so firm, so steadfast that—for that moment at least—I believed what she had said. But there were many times when I was sorely plagued with doubt, and cursed the witch who had convinced her that we could do this thing, and counted myself a lunatic for agreeing to it.

I could not bear to look up the cliff, could not bear to look anywhere. I fair shook with fear, I don't mind confessing; and I think I wept as well, for the grief that the smell of dragon fumes and death awoke in me. It was the same stench I had smelled in my own village, after all had been destroyed. For strength I gazed at Jing-wei's face, and saw it still serene, her expression unreadable.

Among her hidden feelings must lie pains as great as any I have borne, for she, too, lost everything, and was a freak in a travelling fair when first I met her. She was called Lizzie then, for even her own name they had taken from her. Mayhap she learned to hide her feelings when she lived inside a cage, poked at by curious children, gawked at, spat at, hated and mocked. It is hard to think that when I first saw her I, too, thought she was not wholly human, but a half-beast with hooves and claws. I know her better now, though I would never claim to know her well. She still is a mystery to me, though we have suffered much, and triumphed much, and together been to hell and back.

But my tale races too far and fast ahead. Mayhap I should begin at the beginning, on that evil night it all started.

I saw the way you rolled your eyes just then, Brother Benedict, and caught the way you dipped your pen, impatient-like, in the pot of ink. Your tolerance, please! Storytelling is new to me, but I shall soon get in the way of it and put my words in better order. I wish that I could write and be my own scribe, then there'd be no need to make this call upon your time. The Abbot knows my story—I told him briefly—and he said Jing-wei and I might remain here at the monastery as guests for as long as it takes for you to write my narrative. He seems to think my tale important, and instructed me to tell it full well, with nothing spared. I told him that I have no alms to pay for hospitality, but he said Jing-wei could help Brother Gregory in the infirmary, mixing medicines and making poultices, and feeding the aged monks; and I'm to work in the kitchen every day between the hour of tierce and noon, to help the cooks get dinner—a decision the Abbot shall soon repent of, I think, when he eats my pastries. And in the afternoons and evenings, so the Abbot said, you and I shall do this work, for what it's worth.

We are ready, then, your pen sharp and inked, and the candles bright enough? I shall begin again, at the beginning.

* * *

My name is Jude, son of Perkin Swinnard, who kept swine in the village of Doran. My adventure began on a night soon after summer's start this year. It was a night I remember well in every detail, for it was my last with my family. I was in a bad humour, unhappy with my lot. I'm ashamed and sorry now for those dark thoughts, but shall confess them to you for the sake of honesty. Also, I think some saint in heaven, with nothing better to do, cast his eye across my thoughts that hour, disapproved of my ingratitude, and decided to stir up my pot.

I was thinking on the unfairness of fate, and how I was destined to be ever feckless with a bow, to be ill-proportioned and unhandsome, and plagued with four sisters all younger than I. In that bleak mood I thought on other misfortunes, too: how I was fated to be ever tongue-tied and bumbling with the fair Prue, whose father was the big-fisted miller, hell-bent on saving her from mortal errors such as myself by making her a nun; fated to spend the rest of my days minding smelly pigs, and my evenings keeping the four plagues out of the fire, out of the well, and out of my mother's way; and, worst of all, fated to fall unknown into my grave, my courage untested, my fame unsung. In short, I considered myself doomed to a life of pigs and plagues, with no Prue, and no escape.

That early summer's eve I was minding the fire, keeping the cauldron, with its leg of salted bacon, boiling, and trying to finish the new boots I was making for myself. They were almost done; I'd made the upper parts, and had only to punch holes through the leather soles and sew the pieces together. The eldest plague, Addy, hovered close, blocking the firelight so I couldn't see, and whining. The next in line, Lucy, was playing on the blankets and furs, spread on the floor, that were our family bed. The twins, barely three summers old, were asleep. In a corner near a rush-light dipped in fat sat my grandfather, near sixty now, and the oldest soul in the village. He was whittling at a bit of wood, his head bent so close to the torch I wondered that he did not catch alight. As always, he muttered to himself, for he had escaped the ecstasies of swineherding by going to war against the Scots, and coming back blind in one eye, and with his wits half gone. In the corner opposite my grandfather were stalled my father's two oxen, munching happily on hay. In the rafters above our heads perched our five hens, safe inside for the night, and clucking softly as they settled down. The evening would have been peaceful, but for Addy.

"You should have given it to me," she said.

"Given you what?" I asked.

"Your old bow," she said, bumping my arm so the mallet missed the awl and smashed my thumb.

I swore, but not so loud that my mother heard. "If you don't give me peace," I warned, "I'll give you the bow and an arrow, too, stuck where you don't want it."

"You can't give me your bow," she said. "You threw it in the duck pond. I saw. Why?"

"You were spying on me, mayhap."

"I meant, why did you throw it away?"

"Because it was a useless bow, never would shoot straight."

"I doubt that was the bow's fault, Jude," said my mother, laughing at me over the leeks she was preparing. "You'll regret throwing it away. You should have sold it."

That had come to my mind, after the bow had sunk beneath

the water. "I have enough money for a new bow, anyway," I said. "I'm going to Rokeby tomorrow, to buy one. Father said there's a man there makes excellent bows. There's a fletcher there, too, so I can buy new arrows as well."

"There's a good saddler in Rokeby," said my grandfather, without looking up from his whittling. "Made the gear for Alfred. Why don't you take Alfred tomorrow, lad? You'd be at Rokeby quick as an arrow. He's a good horse, Alfred."

Alfred was the horse he rode to war, and which died under him in battle forty years past.

"And who will look after the pigs, if you're not here?" asked my mother.

"Father said he will, tomorrow. 'Tis all arranged. I leave at dawn, and will be back afore the dark."

Addy tugged at my sleeve, and I knew what was coming next. "Take me with you!" she pleaded.

"Aye, and further if you like," I replied. "I'll take you all the way to Constantinople, and leave you there."

"Where's that?" she asked, full of hope. Perchance she longed for adventure as much as I did.

"It's where the knights went on crusades," I said. "Where the heathens skin children alive and use their hides to make fine parchment for clever scribes to write upon."

"And how is it that you know such things, Jude?" asked my mother, with a shrewd look.

I bent low over my new boots, and kept my peace. If she knew I heard it from a travelling minstrel in the alehouse, she would box my ears until my head buzzed like a beehive. She had fists quicker than the miller's; that I knew right well.

"They do not skin children," said Addy, sulking. "Anyway, 'tis silly, you buying a new bow. Your aim will still be bad."

"I can shoot an acorn from forty paces," said I.

"No you can't. You shot at Jack Plowman's barn the other day, and missed."

I pinched her rump—I'd found this was an inconspicuous way to punish her—and went on with my hammering.

"Anyway," whispered Addy spitefully, refusing to cry, "I heard Prue tell Kitty Smythe that you were built like a dumb ox, with brains to match!"

Fortunately for Addy, our father arrived home at that moment, and put upon the hearth the rabbits he had trapped.

"Can I have the skins?" I asked, thinking to trim my boots with fur.

He did not hear; nor did he greet us with his usual cheerfulness, but sat on the dirt floor beside me to warm his hands by the fire, for though the days were warm the nights were cool. His were large hands, steady and strong like the rest of him. His face was ordinary, square-jawed and snub-nosed—like mine, from what I have seen of it in the millpond on a still day. I wished I were like him inside as well: calm and fearless, slow to anger, and fair-minded. I confess I am not; an impatient humour rules me, and a tendency to take whichever way is easiest, especially if my hide is endangered.

"I heard news," he said. "Bad news."

Addy was silent for once, and my mother's hands were very still upon the vegetables. My father went on: "Thornhill was razed to the ground yester-eve." His voice broke, and I looked away from him. His only brother was in that village, with his wife and ten rowdy offspring. My father continued, very quiet: "Everything was destroyed, animals, houses, the windmill, the church. The wheat was burned, the fields for miles around scorched black. None survived."

I put the mallet down on the hearth, the leather sole with it. We all waited for him to go on, and the only sounds in the room were the crackling of the fire and the smooth scraping of my grandfather's knife upon the piece of wood. My father sighed deeply and ran his hands through his hair and down across his face. His skin was grey and his whiskers, unplucked for days, stuck out very black. For the first time in my life, I saw him cry.

"Some said it were the Scots," my father went on, after a while. "But there were no hoofprints reported, and no soldiers have been seen. And the people who had fled, who were found lying dead in the charred fields . . . Well, it is said they had no arrows in them, no sign they were slain by human weapons, though they were burned beyond recognition."

My mother sat down suddenly upon a stool. Lucy and Addy went to her, but she did not put her arms around them. She sat like one struck dumb, her face the colour of bleached cloth.

"Fire fell from the skies," said my grandfather, his head still bent over his carving. His voice was quavering and cracked, and it rose as he became more excited, and he carved deeper and deeper into his wood, ruining his work. "It burned all and sundry, rich and poor, women and men, priests and heretics. Not that it mattered with the heretics, of course. And after the fire came the wind, huge tempests that blew the smoke all over Christendom, and killed everyone who looked on it. It was a pestilence, a judgement from the Almighty."

"That wasn't fire then," said my father, very quiet. "That was the Black Death. It was a sickness, not a fire."

"Aye, but they say it started with fire," said grandfather, looking up, his face red and overwrought. "It started over the seas, in the far-off Eastern realms, and was carried here in the ships, blown by ungodly winds, and it planted its evil seeds in the ports, and spread like poison across—"

"'Tis not the Black Death that wiped out Thornhill yesterday," said my father. "I remember the pestilence, how people sickened and died, so many in number that the churchyards were full, and we buried the dead in pits out in the fields. This is different. There were no sick in Thornhill. Not from what I heard. There were no bodies, save a few charred remains. Those . . . those had been partly devoured. And a strange smell hung in the air. So they said."

Grandfather stared at him, still whittling furiously with his knife. Suddenly the knife slipped, and sliced a deep cut across his hand. "There's another kind of death," he said, not even noticing. "My father spoke of it. And that *was* fire—fire and smoke from hell itself."

My mother fetched a cloth and a bowl of water, and knelt to bathe his cut. My grandfather babbled on about beasts with wings and fiends from hell, then he started weeping and muttering to our grandmother, though she died afore I was born. Soundless, my mother cried as she bound his bleeding palm.

Addy and Lucy started whimpering, which awoke the twins, who in their turn set up a howling fit to wake the dead. I confess I felt like bawling myself, from the awful fear and grief that fell on me. I looked at my father, seeking strength there; but he was staring into the fire, his face white like my mother's, and he shook all over, as if he looked upon Lucifer himself. It was the first time I had ever seen him afraid. The fear spread through our house like smoke, thick and choking. The four plagues wailed louder, as if they felt it, too, and the noise unnerved me. It must have nettled my father as well, for he cried of a sudden: "For Heaven's love! Give me peace!" Grandfather stopped babbling, but the plagues only howled louder. My father got up and went out, slamming the door behind him, making the flames leap, and smoke and ashes swirl.

My eyes watered from the smoke, and I wiped them on my sleeve and picked up the mallet again. I tried not to look at my mother, but from the corner of my eye I saw her head bent, her face streaked with tears. She finished binding my grandfather's hand, then went to the four plagues and rocked them gently against her, though they went on bawling heartily and would not be comforted.

The evening was ruined. I finished my boots but, although they were fine, there was no satisfaction in them. Neither was there excitement in tomorrow's journey. Three summers I had worked for our neighbours in their harvest fields, earning pennies to buy a better bow. Now the precious coins gave me no pleasure, and when I lay in bed with my mother and sisters, it was not expectation for the morrow that kept me awake, but a deepened sense of gloom. I was still awake when my father returned, near dawn. He stank of ale, and I supposed he had been drinking with one of our neighbours. He did not come to bed, but threw more wood on the dwindling fire and sat by it, his head in his hands.

Sunlight crept around the tattered edges of the oiled cloths across our windows, and birds sang. My mother got out of bed and began to make barley cakes. Feigning sleep, I saw my father take her in his arms, and whisper to her. They wept together, very quiet.

Later we all sat on the dirt by the fire and tried to eat the barley cakes she had made. We did not speak. My mind tumbled with thoughts of kinfolk all burned alive, their village with them, and a looming fear I could not name.

TWO

THE VILLAGE OF ROKEBY was some ten miles from my home, but I enjoyed the walk. The day was hot, so I did not take my cloak, only my purse tied to my belt alongside my knife and a small skin of ale to slake my thirst. On my feet were my new boots, mighty comfortable and looking grand, though I say so myself.

My heart grew lighter, the further I got from home and the woe that beset my family. My mother had cried, begging me not to go. My father had looked very grim, and told me to take great care and keep my ears open in Rokeby for further news. I resolved to do no such thing; I had had enough of misery for one day.

To my pleasure I found a fair on the Rokeby village green. It was one of those travelling carnivals with a puppet theatre, stalls selling pies and candied fruits, and pavilions with pictures painted on the sides, describing the wonders within. There were flute players, a man playing the bagpipes, people dancing, wrestlers, and noisy games of blindman's buff. Adding to the noise were the usual solitary travellers who went to every fair: traders calling out their wares, salt and iron peddlers, ballad singers, and healers with herbs promising cures for everything from carbuncles to witches' curses. I was tempted to spend some of my precious pennies, but went on to the village and sought out the man who made bows, and the fletcher. Then, with my new bow across my back and a fine quiver bristling with arrows—and even some change jingling in my purse—I went back to the fair.

I bought an apple tart to eat. The woman who sold it to me admired my bow. "You ought to test your skill," she said, pointing to a small crowd across the ground, where a bright target board had been set up. "There's Richard the archer over there, giving a silver florin to anyone who can shoot better than himself. Go and challenge him. A strong lad like you must be right cunning with a bow."

I could see Richard well. He was skilled, graceful to watch, his aim perfect.

"I think not," I replied. "'Twould be a shame to win his silver from him so early in the afternoon."

I wandered off, eating my apple tart, past brightly painted pavilions advertising a fire-eater, a strong man, the world's fattest lady, a bear and a wildcat, and other such marvels. But it was the swordsman's pavilion that caught my eye, with its painting of a well-muscled man wielding a mighty sword. A performance was about to begin, so I paid a coin to the lad at the entrance, and went in.

It was crowded inside, but I squeezed through the throng to the front, where a stage was set up. People talked while we waited, and I heard a man say: "The swordsman is the grandson of a knight, so 'tis said. His sword slew dragons, once. I'll warrant it'll be used again, that blade, afore this summer's out."

"Aye—used to slice out your foolish tongue," muttered the woman next to him, and people laughed.

"'Tis nothing to jest about," said a crone, wrinkled and bent like a willow branch. "I've seen the past, and I've seen the future, and they both are full of fire a-falling from the skies."

"Mind your tongue, Mother Gloomhart," said someone else. "'Tis foolish, what you say. And 'tis dangerous, spreading direful thoughts."

"There's more than thoughts spreading through this place," said another woman. "My Tomas saw a devil running down the lane yesterday. Had a pointed tail and horns and red skin, it did, and left an evil smell behind it."

"Mayhap it farted," said a lad, and some laughed, though his mother boxed his ears.

Then a man climbed onto the platform, bearing a great sword in his right hand, and we all were silent. He announced: "Tybalt is my name. I do be the grandson of the knight Sir Allun, last of the dragon slayers. This sword has won great victories, and has spilled the blood of many winged beasts. Watch and wonder, for the bravery and skill of noble knights runs in my veins!"

He held the sword blade upright, very still so that we all, as one man, held our breath to see what he would do; then very slowly he swung it downwards and around, in a great and deadly circle before him. Faster it moved, and faster, whistling through the air until I could not see the blade at all, but many blades, circling him with silver light. It moved above his head, then to his left, then his right. Graceful, he moved with it, and it was like a dance, beautiful and marvellous to behold.

The sword flew high in the air, then came down, spinning; we fell back, trampling one another, afraid. But he caught it, and laughed. We all laughed and cheered, applauding him mightily. He bowed, then looked down upon us all, his eyes alight like fire. He had a powerful face, fierce and handsome and darkly bearded. "I need a man," he said. "Someone brave and steadfast, not afraid to face death itself."

No one moved, excepting that men looked down at their feet, or got busy of a sudden whispering to their wives. Tybalt invited several up onto the stage, but each one declined. Then the swordsman's eyes found me.

"Now there's a big brave lad!" he said.

I blushed deep and looked behind me, hoping he spoke of someone else. The woman next to me chuckled and shoved me forward. I had no choice; amid laughter and friendly jests I was hoisted ungracefully onto the stage. During the jostle my quiver tipped and all my arrows clattered across the floor. Embarrassed, I scrambled to pick them up, and heard guffaws from the onlookers. Tybalt put down his sword and crouched to help. Solemn-faced, he put the arrows back in the quiver, then helped me take off my bow and placed it with the quiver out of the way. Then he picked up his sword again and we both stood facing the crowd. He was head and shoulders taller than I, and slender-built, for all his strength.

"What's your name, lad?" he asked, putting an arm across my shoulders.

"Jude," said I. My voice shook, like the rest of me, though I struggled to look coolheaded.

"Is your lady mother watching us, Jude?"

"Nay. I'm of Doran, here only for today. I came alone."

"Then this is a lucky day for you"—he smiled—"and for me. For once I can test a lad's nerve without his mother scolding me."

The people laughed again, doubtless relieved to be safe while a stranger faced death for their amusement. I swallowed hard. I don't think I had ever been so afraid, except once when I came close to kissing Prue.

"First," said Tybalt, "we've a few doubts to dispel, which these good folk might entertain. Take the sword, Jude." He held it out to me, the blade still upright, steady in his hands.

I took the weapon, and almost dropped it. By God's bones, 'twas heavy! I staggered at the weight of it, and the people laughed again, thinking I acted the fool.

"Hold the blade straight up," Tybalt said quietly. "Keep the weight balanced, 'twill be easier." Then he said aloud, so all could hear: "There has been a suggestion, Jude, that this sword is merely a harmless wooden toy painted to look as steel. Is it wood, think you?"

"'Tis a mite heavy for wood," I said, struggling to hold the sword upright. My arms ached, and I was afeared I'd drop the thing and cut off someone's feet, or worse. Seeing my struggle, Tybalt took the weapon back. He spun it in a slow arc, and I scuttled back, making the people hoot and laugh again.

Tybalt looked across the crowd, then said to one of the elderly women, "Give me an apple from your basket, good mother." An apple was thrown up onto the stage. He caught it deftly, then gave it to me. "Throw it high, straight up," he said, "then stand back, quick."

I did as he commanded, and as the apple came down he swung his blade. The fruit fell to the floor, sliced clean into two, and I picked up the pieces and held them out for the people to see. There were whistles and cheers.

"I see you're an archer, Jude," Tybalt said, when they had settled down. "A hunter. You know, then, how to move slow and quiet, how to stand motionless, and hardly breathe?"

"I've not hunted much," I confessed.

"But you can stand still, Jude?"

"Aye."

He took me to the centre of the stage and stood me so I faced the people. They looked wrought up, eager. I suppose it is how they watch at a hanging, all gaping and gawking. Tybalt pressed my arms closer to my sides, tucking my elbows against my belt. I stared across the heads of the onlookers and tried to calm my thudding heart. Tybalt stood beside me, his sword raised. "Remember how you stand when about to shoot a stag," he said, very soft. "You do not move, nor breathe. Stand like that for me. Now."

I froze like a hare when it first hears the hunter. I was aware of the soft whirring of the blade, slow at first, then fast. It whistled about me, a silver wind across my skin, now beside me, now in front, now above. I felt a movement on my hair, light as thistle-down, then something black brushed my face. It was a lock of my own hair, tumbling to the floor. I heard a woman scream, and others gasped. The people, the pavilion walls, were misty as a dream. Nought was real, save that steel-cold wind. It swept my scalp again, and another tangle fell. I remember thinking, in that uncanny calm betwixt terror and trust, of my mother, and how she would give a hundred barley cakes to witness this. She used to sit on me to cut my hair, and of late had given up the battle altogether. And here I was, being shorn half bald, without a word of protest! She could hire Tybalt, and have the four plagues trimmed as well, right quick, and my father. More hair fell. And then the steel slowed, and stopped.

I looked at Tybalt. Sweat poured off him, and his shirt was wet.

"Brave lad," he said, with that dark smile of his, and I fair bristled with pride. "I've had noble soldiers flinch from my blade. Give a cheer for Jude of Doran, good village folk. You have a brave man among you this day." There was applause again, stamping and cheering and whistling. Dizzy with success, I was helped down off the stage. As I left, someone called that I had forgot my bow and arrows, and a man chuckled as he handed them to me.

Outside, I slung my quiver and bow across my back, passed my hand across my oddly shaven scalp, and walked with my head high. Someone in the crowd bumped into me and cursed me heartily, and I remember feeling greatly affronted by his disrespect. Could he not tell—could none in that crowd tell—that I, Jude of Doran, had that very hour faced death, and not been moved? I wanted to shout my valour to the skies. I tell you, Brother Benedict, if ever my soul flew and touched the face of God, it was then. I'll warrant all your prayers and petitions never got you nearer paradise than Tybalt's sword got me, that day.

Talking of paradise, it must be almost time for prayers. Take your rest, Brother, for we wrote much yesterday, and 'twould be a calamity to wear you out this early in my narrative, afore I've got to the enthralling part.

THREE

REETINGS, BROTHER BENEDICT! Writing already, I see, and my day's narrative not even begun! Ah—I can guess why. Yester-eve the Abbot asked me about the stuff called paper, that the Chinese write upon, and I wondered how he heard of it. Now I remember that I mentioned paper to you yesterday afore you picked up your pen, while you unrolled the new parchment. I'll warrant you told the Abbot of it, and that now he thinks there might be other pearls of wisdom in these pleasantries of mine. I suppose he instructed you henceforth to write down every word. 'Tis a waste of good ink, Brother; I swear I'll not drop any pearls until you hold your pen, ready and inked. What? Still writing anyway? It comes of swearing obedience to your Abbot, I suppose. Well then, without further ado, on with the tale.

My father had told me to listen for news at Rokeby. Though I had forgot his instruction, I did hear news as I was about to leave. I overheard two women speaking, and got the words "burned to the ground" and pricked up my ears.

"Aye," one of the women was saying, her voice hushed, "everything was destroyed, they said. The whole of Wicklan, the fields and all. 'Tis the beginning of the Day of Judgement, for sure."

Wicklan? They spoke of Thornhill, surely, that was razed yesterday? I moved nearer, and listened as they continued.

"Only the priest escaped," went on the first woman. "He hid in the crypt beneath the church, and came out three days later to find that all was ash and blackened stone. He ran all the way to the next town, arrived babbling like an idiot, his hair gone white overnight. He said he saw what did it. Saw it coming, flying down from the sky with fire pouring—"

"Hush!" whispered her friend, glancing at the children gathered about their skirts. She added, in a brighter tone: "Let's go and see the bear, Mary. Mayhap they will bait it with a pack of hounds. That will cheer us up and entertain the little ones."

They wandered off, leaving me disturbed, my new-won joy gone down a notch or two. As I passed the last pavilion, the picture on it caught my eye. It was an evil image: a being half human, half animal, with outlandish scarlet robes, devilish slanting eyes, and tiny hooves. Craving distraction from the news I had heard, and not a little curious, I joined the line that was beginning to form outside. A brawny man was taking money as people filed in, and a lad stood beside him shouting: "See Lizzie Little-feet, curiosity from the great Empire of China! Discover heathen rituals! See foreign costumes of priceless silk! Hear the mysterious language of Babble!"

Slowly we shuffled forward, one by one entering the dimness.

I was one of the first in, so I got a good place again, right near the stage. Afore long the pavilion was near full, and there was a great deal of jostling and pushing behind me. Children were grizzling to be picked up so they could see, though there was nothing yet to be seen, save an empty stage and a large bolted wooden box painted with hideous faces. The box was guarded by a man, who was shortly joined by Tybalt himself. The swordsman recognised me, and gave me a grin and a wink.

Behind me, a boy asked if the freak was dangerous, and whether it had two heads. "I don't know, son," the lad's father replied. "But she's a wicked heathen, so she'll have horns, more like, and hoofed feet."

Other people laughed, though there was little mirth in it. Then the pavilion entrance was closed, putting us all in darkness. Instantly there was silence. Of a sudden I was afraid, thinking on another freak I had seen in another fair, long ago when I was small. That freak had been hideously misshapen, his face disfigured beyond any semblance to a human being, and I had been in terror of him, though he was heavily chained. Could this monster be worse?

A torch was set aflame, lighting the box and the faces of the men bending over it. People pressed forward, and I was crushed so hard against the stage, I had to put my hands on the edge of it to brace myself. The faces on the painted box were so close I could have spat on them.

The box was unbolted, the lid thrown back. Ghost-like in the semidarkness, a figure rose from within. It raised its arms, there was a shimmer of red silk, and the torch was passed quick beneath its face. The face was small, human, yet different. Only for a moment I saw it—saw the alien brown features, goblin-like and freakish, with dusky wild hair and coal-black almond-shaped eyes—then the torch was whipped away. Truth to tell, I was disappointed. Hardly a freak, this, compared with the other I had seen!

The person was lifted out and placed upright on the stage. Small it was, half lost within folds of scarlet silk, teetering like a child barely able to stand. Then it lifted its shining hem, and the torchlight passed close by its feet. They were small, far too small for human feet, and I thought they must be devil's hooves. Then the freak began to walk. Up and down the platform it walked, not quickly, but with tiny limping steps, as if its feet were chained closely together. Its head was bent, its hands folded at its waist. I watched, appalled and entranced. Was it human, or was it some alien half-thing, unnatural and demonic? Just then the freak stopped hobbling and turned to face us all. In the leaping flame-light from the torch I saw its face again, and realised, with a start, that it was a maid.

"Speak, O Heathen One," commanded Tybalt, holding the torch flame by her head.

For a moment she hesitated, swaying as if her tiny feet were hardly able to support her, though she was slight enough to be blown away by the wind. Then she opened her mouth and chanted a bizarre little song, her voice high and lilting, making words as strange as spells. When she had finished, she very politely bowed low. People cheered and clapped, though I did not. I don't know what I felt—fear, or fascination, or pity. She was like a changeling, a strange brown elf-child, enchanting and fragile. Some of the people standing close called her a hobgoblin and spat at her.

Tybalt commanded the freak to do something else, and she sat on a stool and took off her tiny shoes. Being close, I noticed that her fingernails were long and curved, like claws. Her feet were bandaged. At another order from her keeper, and with the torch held close to her, she removed the bindings. Her feet were grotesque, misshapen clumps with the toes and heels curved down and inwards, almost touching underneath. And they were flat, shapeless, as if the bones had all been broke.

"They've been bound up like that since she were a little child," announced Tybalt. "That's what they do in the barbarian land she's from. It's to keep the women in their place, you see. To stop them a-wandering, and gossiping, and getting up to mischief. A very sensible custom we would do well to take on, here."

Some of the men chuckled, shouting agreement, and their wives scolded them.

"That fine garment she wears," Tybalt went on, "it's silk, made from worms."

People roared with laughter and disbelief.

"True!" he cried, smiling a little. "You've heard of the East, of the Silk Road, of old Cathay, and the Orient, land of silk and fabulous furs. Well, that's where she's from: China. She's an Easterling. Our kings and queens wear purple finery brought along that famous Silk Road from her far land. And more than silk is brought: fine treasures, idols of silver and gold, and all manner of jewels. A long way she's come, this barbarian maid, to entertain and educate you gentlefolks. Heathen she is, prays to golden idols and devils and all things wicked and forbidden. Her people are uncivilised, backward. They live in ignorance and heinous sin. You'll never see the likes of her anywhere else in our land, so look well."

Several people made the sign of the cross, doubtless fearing that the very presence of the heathen maid might breathe evil over them. An echo of my grandfather's ravings came to me: something about the Black Death coming from the East, filling the sky with fire and blowing to England on evil winds. Had she seen the fire, this tiny freak? Is that why her eyes were narrowed and slanted—to shut out the light and the heat from the fiery skies?

"How did you come by her?" called out a woman.

"Well, that'd be telling a great secret," said Tybalt. "But you may be sure, she's rare and precious."

Other questions were asked, not all answered. During them the maid remained very still, her hands folded in her lap, her small, strange face uplifted. Around me, people began to leave. Tybalt departed, doubtless to his own tent for another breathtaking performance with his sword, leaving the other man to stand guard. I stayed, I know not why, looking at the freakish girl upon the stool. Slowly she bent and bound the linen strips about her feet again, then pulled on her tiny shoes. When she raised her head, I alone was left.

As her gaze met mine, her lofty look disappeared, and to my surprise she smiled.

"You let Tybalt play his sword about you," she said. Her soft voice was mildly accented. Her words, and the expression on her face, startled me.

"How do you know?" I asked. It felt odd, exchanging words with her.

"Your hair," she said.

"Ah." I touched the top of my head, feeling the bristles. "Well . . ." Tongue-tied again, as always, with a maid—even a freakish one.

"He has done that but few times before," she said.

"Done what?" I asked.

"Shaved off hair. Most people tremble so, he dares not do it. You must have been right brave."

"Not brave," I said, and felt my face grow hot. "Scared stiff, more like."

Again she smiled, then her guard roughly picked her up and carried her out an exit at the back of the tent. As they went outside I glimpsed a cage with a dark grey canvas across the top.

I was left alone in the silence. A strange feeling fell on me. I cannot say 'twas fate, or a foreknowing, but it was something akin to it. I knew that we should meet again.

Do you need rest, Brother? You yawn—a yawn brought on by the evening's warmth and the mead, I hope, and not because my tale is dull. I thought that I was getting into the swing of it quite well. Ah—I just noticed—your candles are near burned out. We'll continue after dinner on the morrow, and I'll tell you what I found when I went home.

ƒOUR

AIL, BROTHER. 'TIS STRAIGHT into the tale today, for this is the hardest part of it for me, and the sooner done, the better.

On the way back to Doran I practised with my new bow: shot at a hare and hit a hill. The wind was stronger than I judged, and sent my arrow amiss. The road seemed longer, too, and it was sunset when I left the woods and began to climb the last rise that lay between my home and me. Most of the time I walked with my head down, watching the road for ruts and holes, but as I left the woods and began to climb the hill I smelled smoke in the air, and raised my eyes. I saw a terrible thing. The brow of the hill still hid my village, but the sky above Doran was black with smoke, spreading high and wide, veiling the low sun.

Disbelief went through me first, and then a fear so deep that I could scarcely breathe. I ran up the hill, stumbling in my haste, half blind with acrid fumes, fine ash, and tears.

Doran was gone. Burned bare. Trees, wheat, farm carts,

ploughs, vegetable plots, sheep, goats, chickens—everything was gone. Only some of the clay block walls of the cottages still stood, and they were black, many cracked and fallen in the heat. Thatched roofs were gone, the little wattle fences between the houses, the wooden sheds where pigs were kept, the ploughs and carts—all gone. I recognised nothing, for everything was black. Even the little lanes had vanished, or I could not make them out with fences and gardens and farm buildings disappeared. There was nothing. Nothing but ash and glowing embers, and smoke. And the stink . . .

I don't remember much of that night. I still have nightmares of running to and fro on the edges of the glowing ash, choking and retching in the smoke, howling for my parents, for little Addy and Lucy and the twins, and Grandfather. In my dreams the air is full of screams and wails, and I suppose they were mine. I could see my home, a blackened husk. I tried to run to it, but the embers and heat and fumes beat me back. The air was full of the smell of roasted meat. And there was another smell, deeper than the smoke, a sulfurous smell that stung my eyes and nose, and tasted bitter in my mouth. I still can taste it, even now.

The next thing I remember clearly is washing my hands at dawn, in the stream that ran to the ruined mill. My palms were blistered, bleeding, covered in black ash. My clothes were filthy, everything was black, and the soles of my boots were scorched. I remember that I washed my face in the stream, and looked up after, expecting to see the village there as it had always been, and Addy running up to vex me with some new game she wanted me to play. Several times I did that, washed and looked up, craving to see Doran again the way it was.

But it was not, and Addy never came.

There was no wind, and the day was hot, uncannily quiet. No birds sang, no cattle lowed, and no crickets chirped. I found one tree at the edge of what had been the south wheat-field. I climbed up and sat there, high in the branches among the ash-laden leaves. Hiding, perchance. Waiting.

From there I could see the layout of the village, and better make out where the houses had been, though much was hard to recognise. Scattered in the ashes, and across the stubble in the charred fields, were distorted piles of blackness. I realised, after staring at them for some time, what they were, and horror so great came over me that I screamed and wept, and curled up into a little ball in the tree, and prayed for death, cursing the mischance that had led me out of the village that day, guilty that they all had died and I had not. Then I slept, evil dreams mingling with the stink of smoke and death.

I awoke with a shout and an almighty crash, and found myself flat on my back on the ground, with human legs all around me. I cried and laughed, thinking they were my own Doran folk, and it had all been a dreadful dream; but then a man bent over me, and I saw that it was Tybalt. I could tell from his face, and from the other faces bending close, that it was no dream. Around me, people were arguing about what caused the fire. Some were saying it had been soldiers; others said it was the wrath of God, or the beginning of Judgement Day. Then someone said the Black Death must have come to Doran, and the people had shut themselves in and burned themselves and all they had, to keep the pestilence from spreading. I lost my wits, I think; I seem to remember howling like a madman, and kicking and biting the people who tried to help me. I refused the food and drink they offered me, even refused to touch my bow and arrows, which a boy had found somewhere. I am ashamed to think how rude I was to them, telling them to sod off and leave me be. Tybalt tried to reason with me, but I swore at him, and in the end he forced me into the long covered wagon he travelled with and slept in, with his family. I fought, and he hit me, I think, for I woke up with a throbbing head and aching jaw, and found myself alone in the wagon, being jolted along the road like a prisoner going to his hanging. My very teeth rattled, my head ached, and my heart was so sore I wept in pity for myself.

And that, Brother Benedict, is how I came to be staying with Tybalt's family, and how I came to meet up again with Lizzie Little-feet.

I have told enough for today, for thinking on these things makes me mortal tired. I'll go for a walk around the monastery gardens, for they are very beautiful, and there is peace in them. Mayhap I'll find Brother Tobit in the vineyard, with his hoe and cheery face and wicked jokes. Did he ever tell you the story about Adam and Eve and how they— By God's bones! Are you writing this down, as well? I'm off!

ƒIVE

ROTHER, I'M HOT WITH HASTE in getting here! I'm sorry I'm late; I've been talking with the monk in charge of the vineyards. He said the grapes are ripe for harvest, and that soon you will all be busy making wine and mead. With a twinkle in his eye, he told me that the Abbot said my pies are not quite to his taste, and henceforth I'm to help in the winery. I knew the Abbot would soon repent of letting me loose in his kitchen! And the winery will suit me well. Are you still bent on writing every word? God's precious heart—it shall take till Christmastide to write my tale! Well, now that you've got the vital stuff down, we'll continue with the story.

They were passing strange, those first days with Tybalt's people, more dream than real. When my anger was spent I slipped into a pit of woe so deep I thought that I would never claw my way out. Tybalt and his family left me mostly to myself. While we travelled I stayed in their wagon, resting on a straw mattress, not caring that only frail crones and giggling maids travelled in the wagon with me. I could not have walked, or ridden a horse even if they gave me one; my strength had fled, as if millstones weighed me down. I spoke to no one, ate little of what they put in front of me, and drank deep of ale, which numbed my pain a bit. When we were camped I slept wrapped in a rug on the ground underneath Tybalt's wagon. Although the weather was warm, I was deadly cold.

I recall that one morning we stopped near a town and there was some debate, between Tybalt and the others, as to whether they should travel on or tarry there. Tybalt owned the fair, and in any discussion his word was always the last. In the end Tybalt and his two sons went to buy bread and extra food, while we stayed outside the city walls, with the horses and wagons. While we waited I heard the church bells tolling, and someone said it was the Feast of Corpus Christi. I thought of all the feast days I had gone to mass in the church of Doran, and of the bright paintings on the church walls, the candles and incense, the familiar rituals, and our old priest chanting the prayers in Latin, which I didn't understand, of course, but loved for the richness of his voice. I enjoyed the feast days, since on them I didn't have to tend the swine, and in the evenings we all danced in the church-yard and sang wild songs the priest disapproved of. Sometimes I had managed to hug Prue's waist.

Alas! There'd be no embracing now, not of her nor anyone else I loved. I was getting myself right woeful, when Tybalt and his sons came back with enough provisions for a siege. They had heard talk in the town, they said, of other villages that were burned, and of survivors, half mad with fear and grief, who swore they had seen a winged beast. The townsfolk were living in fear, and every day at sundown they extinguished all their lamps and fires, to keep the town hid in the dark.

"There are warnings spoken at every gate and tavern door," said Tybalt's elder son. He was Richard, the archer I had seen at the fair. "People are advised not to travel unless it's necessary, and then to keep away from open fields and roads. And they're told not to light fires at night, for that is when the dragon hunts, and it may be drawn to the smell of cooking meat."

"They're all mistook," said Tybalt. "The dragons were killed, every one, near sixty summers past. My own grandfather slew the last of them, and searched for seven years after through the caves and the mountains, destroying all the eggs. My father helped him in those searches, and spilled some dragon yolk himself, so he told me. However, something's causing fires. Myself, I think it's those mad Scots, riding down from the north and plundering our villages and setting everything afire, just to taunt us. We'll not journey on the roads while they're about, but settle in the woods and wait for the savagery to stop."

I remembered what my father had said about there being no hoofprints around his brother's village after it were burned; and there had been no hoofprints in the fields around Doran, either. I thought Tybalt's notion wrong, but said nothing.

Tybalt commanded us to unpack the sacks of provisions and share them fairly. That done, we journeyed on.

For several days we camped in one place in a forest, beside a river. During the day I sat by the water and did nothing. Once some children came and stood in a row in front of me, grinning and giggling. A girl carried a little stone, which she threw at me, striking me on the temple. I felt blood trickle down my cheek, but did not move.

"Mad boy, mad boy," she said, and bent to pick up a clod of earth. Then she began a silly rhyme, which the others took up.

> *"Jude of Doran spent a florin*
> *At the Rokeby fair,*
> *Drank from a flagon while a dragon*
> *Burned his village bare."*

Over and over they sang it, throwing stones and dirt at me, until Tybalt roared at them and they ran off, laughing and shrieking, to torment the freak.

I stayed where I was by the river, and sank deeper into misery. Tybalt came and sat by me. After a time he said, with gentleness: "I know you have a brave heart, Jude, though it's been sorely tested of late. But it's time to put an end to woe. Some matters can't be mended, and we have to go on as best we may."

I knew he spoke fair enough, yet I could not banish the memory of my charred village, and could not stop thinking of how people must have panicked, fleeing through the wheat until even that was set afire. Images blazed through my mind, horrific, unbearable. I bent my head on my arms again, and felt Tybalt put a hand upon my shoulder.

"Don't dwell on it, lad," he said. "When you're ready, work will help. It'll help us, as well as yourself."

That evening I drank too much ale for my good, and got up in the night to be sick in the river. When I turned to go back a man stood there, his bow drawn and an arrow in place. I could not see his face, for although it was a moonlit night, we were under trees and the shadows were black. I thought of robbers, and near spewed again, from sheer fright; but then he spoke and I realised he was Richard.

"'Tis you," he said, "wasting my father's ale."

"Sorry," said I.

"Aye, so you ought to be," he muttered. We were standing close, and I could see the bitter twist of his mouth and his narrowed eyes. He was tall and well-favoured, like his father. "My father rescued you," he said, "because he thought you had courage, and that you were an archer and would help me hunt to keep his people fed. You're a sorry disappointment, Jude of Doran."

His opinion wasn't worth a turd to me, but I dared not tell him so. I asked, careless-like, "You're hunting tonight?"

"Nay. I'm keeping watch." As he said it he glanced at the skies above the river. I followed his gaze, but saw nought save stars and a thin crescent moon.

"What do you watch for?" I asked. "Marauding Scots?"

"The winged beast," he replied, his voice hushed, his eyes still on the stars. "They say the dragons were exceeding beautiful, for all their deadliness."

"They also say the dragons are dead and gone. Your own father says that."

"He's mistook. A dragon has survived, I know it. And I'd give half my life to see the creature."

"If you do see a dragon, you might well give half your life," I said. "Mayhap all of it."

He gave me a look then that, if a witch had given it, would have withered me to a toad. "You're a craven fool, Jude of Doran," he said. "You forget whose blood runs in my veins. No beast has the power to strike fear into me, whether or not it has wings and spits fire. But you—you're afraid of your own name. You waste your days pining away like a weakling maid, no good to anyone. If I alone were spared out of a whole village, I'd be looking for the reason why, and being glad for it. You don't deserve your good fortune."

"Good fortune?" I cried, so loud that he hushed me, for people were sleeping all around. *"Good fortune?"*

"Aye," he said, bitter-soft. "Good fortune."

He spat on the ground and walked away, his footsteps silent, true hunter's steps.

For most of that night I lay awake, haunted by his words. But though I thought till my head ached, I could find no reason why I alone was left alive. On the morrow, still sunk in grief, I went back to sitting by the river, in the shade of a tree. The day was hellish hot—a foretaste of the uncanny heat that would last all summer long. Some later blamed the heat, and the dried-up ponds and wells, for the terrible spread of the fires and the utter devastation of the villages that were struck.

Later that morning Richard crept up behind me and hit me over the head with four dead hares. While I sprawled in the dust, he said, "Earn your keep. Go and feed the animals."

So I did, giving the bear and wildcat two corpses each. The cat ate hers in a moment, but the bear lay panting in the heat and did not even lift its head. There was dried foam about its mouth, and its eyes were glazed. Neither beast had water. While there I noticed that the cover on the freak's cage had been folded back, and she was hunched in one corner, rocking, her head bent and her arms about her knees. The floor of her cage was covered in rotting grass, and the red dress she had worn for her performance in the fair was rolled in a bundle in one corner. She wore a muck-stained shift and no shoes, but her feet were tightly bound in rags. In another corner was a bucket, near to overflowing, which she used as a privy, and near the cage door a bowl she must have used for food. It had maggots in it. There was a cleaner bowl, too, that I suppose was for water, though it was empty then. There were blowflies everywhere, even in her hair, though she made no move to brush them off. Her cage stank, bad almost as the bear's.

Curious, I went and stood in front of her. She did not notice me at first, but went on rocking, back and forth, back and forth. Suddenly she looked up, and I saw that she was crying. I wanted to flee, to have no part of her misery, for my own was heavy enough; but I stayed, mayhap because she once had smiled on me and called me brave.

Of a sudden I had a disturbing thought. Feed the animals, Richard had said. Had he by chance meant Lizzie Little-feet as well?

"What do they give you to eat?" I asked.

She turned her face away towards the trees, and did not reply. Her skin was begrimed with dirt, sweat, tears, and snot, and I looked again at her maggoty bowl and filthy floor, and almost retched. I wished I had never heard her speak. It would be easier to think she had no reason, no feelings.

I repeated my question and this time she replied, though she still would not look at me. "Nothing," she said. "They've not fed me since the fair." Her voice was low and cracked, and she must have been suffering a cruel thirst.

"I'll ask Tybalt for some food for you," I said.

Tybalt was crouching near his wagon steps, lighting a fire for noonday dinner, and Richard was skinning a hare. Tybalt's younger son, a boy of eleven summers, was skinning a squirrel. The carcasses of two wild swine lay nearby, skinned and threaded ready on a spit. I wondered if Richard had permission to hunt on this land, from the manor-lord who owned it, or whether he had poached.

"Can I have some bread for Lizzie?" I asked.

Tybalt looked up from the kindled fire and grinned. His face was bathed in sweat. "'Tis good to see that you are done with woe," he said. "I'd be grateful if you'd feed the freak, and give her water, and clean out her cage. It's Richard's task to mind her, but he's been busy hunting to feed us all while we've been on the road." He took a key from a bunch he carried at his belt, and gave it to me. "Lock her cage carefully, after. I've lost count of the times she's tried to escape, though she's never got far on her crippled feet. Ask my wife for bread and cheese for her, and see if there's some fish left over from last night."

Tybalt's wife was Kitty, and she was little and bony, and not a friendly soul. But she gave me some bread and cheese for Lizzie, and I scraped the mould from both as I took it back. I passed it through the bars to her, then tried not to watch as she stuffed it into her mouth. I unlocked her cage and picked up her bowls, then locked the cage and took the bowls to the river and scoured them with sand. Both I filled with water, thinking how thirsty she must be. I had to unlock the cage to give her the water. She fair snatched one of the bowls from my hands, pouring the water down her throat so fast she spilled more than she drank. "Leave this other one till later," I said, "else you'll make yourself sick."

As I lifted her down to the ground, she asked me my name. I told her and she said, with a shadow of a smile, "Jude the brave, and Jude the kind."

"Jude the useless," I said, and she smiled in truth. Then she lay facedown in the grass, sniffing, and scraping her long nails into the dirt. At first I feared she had lost her wits, then I realised that the earth was sweet to her, after the cage floor. Using a branch, I swept out her cage. I kept an eye on her, half expecting her to get up and hobble away, but she stayed near the cages, pushing grass and flowers through the bars to the bear and cat, and talking to the beasts in her own language. I emptied her privy bucket in the river and rinsed it as best I could. I was put in mind of looking after my father's swine, and shook my head, half amused, thinking myself still doomed to muck. I washed the floor of her cage, then sat with her in the warm grass while it dried.

Behind us people were cooking their midday dinner over little fires ringed with river stones because of the dryness of the forest floor. I glanced at the wagons; they were placed in a large circle, with Lizzie's cage together with the cages of the cat and bear. The cooking-fires were on the flat bit of forest floor within the circle, and there was friendly talk, and children playing in the dust, and dogs running about barking. We were not in a clearing, but here the trees were thinner, still giving shade, and we could hear the bubbling of the river not far away. The water sounded tempting in the heat. I looked at Lizzie. She was brushing flies from her face and wrists, and her skin was slick with sweat. Her nose was smudged with dirt, from when she sniffed the ground.

"'Tis a pity to put such a filthy creature back in a clean cage," I said. "Would you like a wash?"

"I'd rather drink my water," she replied.

"I didn't mean a wash in your water bowl. I meant, in the river."

A slow smile spread across her face, full of surprise and mischief and delight, like the smiles Addy used to give to me, those few times when I agreed to play a game. It broke my heart, that smile; and it mended it. I picked Lizzie up in my arms and ran with her between the cooking-fires, past the startled people, down to the river. We both were crowing like overjoyed roosters, while I held her close and swept her back and forth, up and down, in the water.

Then there was a bellow behind us, and I looked around to see Tybalt standing there, most of the fair folk gathered behind him.

"By God's body, lad!" he roared, red with rage. "Bring her out—now!"

I carried her up, and felt her arms tight about my neck again, her heart hammering against my breast. My own hammered, too, I don't mind confessing. Never had I seen a man so wild, not even the miller. I felt guilty, and knew not why. Dripping water, I climbed the bank and stood by him. "She was not in any harm," I said. "She was washing."

"You could have drowned her!" he shouted. "She's what draws the crowds, at this fair. Her, and my sword. Put her back in the cage, and mind you lock it. And give me back the key, you mad fool."

In front of them all I carried Lizzie back to her prison. My boots squelched, for I had not stopped to take them off, and my clothes were heavy with water. Everyone was staring, children and adults alike, as if I had two heads and a tail. God's bones, I thought, they'll have *me* in a cage as well, soon—a lunatic to show, besides the freak! I was shaking, afraid of Tybalt and wary of his people, but Lizzie made little chortling sounds, and I realised she was laughing.

"Ah—that were grand, Jude!" she sighed, as I sat her down in the doorway of her cage. "It were better than the time the bear escaped."

I pulled up armfuls of sweet grass and spread them over the floor of her cage. Then I unwrapped the dripping bindings from her feet and hung the strips over a top bar of her cage to dry. I held her wounded feet in my hands, and pity swept over me. Her feet must long ago have been smashed, for there were no bones left whole to give them form. Her toes had been turned under for so long that the toenails had grown and pierced the flesh underneath. It must have been agony for her to walk. "Is it true, what Tybalt said about your feet?" I asked. "Are they broken like this to stop you from walking and wandering?"

"Nay," she said. "It was to keep them beautiful. Only tiny feet are beautiful."

"Who said so?"

"An emperor, many generations ago, in my land. He liked little feet, and commanded that all women highborn must have little feet. In my country we cannot marry well if we have ugly feet. There only peasants have big feet, since they must walk every day to the fields to work."

"You are highborn?"

"Aye." She frowned, looking at her cage. "It is more curse than favour to me."

"Who did this, Lizzie? Who broke your feet?"

She looked away again, her eyes shimmering. "My mother and her mother," she said, whispering. "Together they crushed my feet with big stones, and bound them tight, and pushed them into tiny shoes."

I leaned on the cage door and looked at her, marvelling at her sufferings. I saw then that, for all her tiny size and child-like slenderness, she had a woman's face, a woman's sorrow in her eyes. I wondered how old she was and looked down at the front of her, where her thin shift clung wet against her body. She had small breasts.

Don't blush so, Brother Benedict. You're old, near thirty I should think, and must surely have noticed bosoms. I have to speak true, the Abbot said. And the truth is that Lizzie was not a child. She doesn't know how old she is, but she told me that her woman's-blood began more than two summers past.

And on that obviously disturbing and astounding note, I shall let you take your rest. I'm off to the gardens again, for a walk afore evening prayers. I didn't see Brother Tobit in the vineyard yester-eve, but found the Abbot instead. He asked how our story goes, and I told him it goes well. At least, I hope it does. He shared with me his dream that one day every soul in our land, man, woman, and child, shall be taught letters and be able to read for themselves. For that, he says, we shall need many books. Well, you and I are making one. I wonder if anyone shall ever read it, besides your worthy self. Mayhap I'd better keep the story seemly, on the chance that they might.

SIX

OOD MORROW, BROTHER! I hope I'm not late again; I've been talking with Jing-wei. She's looking after Father Matthew in the infirmary. He's near ninety years old, and crotchety, and he wets his bed every hour. He makes her chant prayers all the time—which she can't do, of course, so she sings to him in Chinese. He's well pleased, and says her Latin's excellent. I hope my story's excellent, as well. So I'd best get on with it, no words to waste!

The next morning I was crouching by the midday fire helping Kitty turn a haunch of deer upon the spit, when Tybalt came and handed me the key to Lizzie's cage. "If you'll swear not to drown her, lad," he said, with a crooked grin, "you may be her keeper for a while. I don't want her neglected, nor starved, nor allowed to get ill."

"I'll not neglect her," I said.

I got a piece of leather thong and tied the key to my belt,

beside the sheath for my knife. For the first time since Doran was destroyed I felt as if I had value again, a purpose to live. I liked Lizzie Little-feet, for all her strangeness. She accepted me, which was more than the rest of Tybalt's people did. She lightened the loneliness in me, and there was an easiness between us I had not known with other maids. Mayhap it was her smallness, which made her seem more like a child than a maid near womanhood, that made me less bumbling in her company; mayhap it was her caged helplessness, or the way her face lit up when I drew near, as little Addy's had. Truth to tell, it was this—her likeness to Addy, more than anything—that eased my pain. I sorely blamed myself that Addy had died, since she had begged that fatal day to go to Rokeby with me; and in a strange way I felt that in Lizzie I was given another chance, a way to mend my wrong. Whatever the reason, I spent more time polishing Lizzie's cage than I needed to, and sometimes shared my meals with her, and we talked comfortably enough. On the third day that I was her keeper, she asked if I would wash her scarlet dress for her, which she used for the performance at the fair. So I did, though the children gawked and cackled and called me Washer-woman. As I spread the gorgeous folds across a branch to dry, I noticed, embroidered on the hem, a curious sign. Worked in midnight blue, it was a pleasing design made of graceful curves and lines, simply but elegantly linked. It was the only thing in blue; the rest of the dress was embroidered richly, but in gold and pink and white.

"What is this?" I asked of Lizzie, whose cage was close, and who was watching me. "Is it a word?"

"It is my name," she replied.

"Lizzie?" I said.

She smiled, putting me in mind of Addy again.

"Nay, dimwit. My name in Chinese. Jing-wei. My mother wrote it there in embroidery silk, that I might not forget."

"You can read?"

"I learned with my brother, on the ship when we left China."

"Your father was a wealthy man, with money for such a journey?"

"Aye. He was a nobleman."

"Why did you come here to England, Lizzie? And how did you end up with Tybalt here, locked in a cage? If your father was wealthy, how did he let such a thing happen?"

"Three questions, Jude, and each reply a tale! What is it you want—the legend of my life?"

"Aye, if you've a mind to give it," I said, smiling. There was something about her eyes, the way they danced, that warmed all of me. Prue's eyes, too, had danced, but in hers laughter had been mockery.

Lizzie smiled again and leaned against the bars of her cage, her arms wrapped about her knees. "Then I'll tell you my life," she said. "It is a gift I give, for all the kindly things you do."

And so I heard her story, and until now have told it to no other soul, for it was her gift to me. But I think you should know it, good Brother, else this tale of mine will hardly be complete. Last night she said I might tell it to you, though she told me her story again and again, and was very particular about it, making me repeat certain parts to make sure I remembered them aright. I'll do my best, and try to tell it in the words she used, and in her way.

This, then, is the maid's tale, of how she came to England,

where she lived here, and how she came to be a freak in a travelling fair.

Until her number-six birthday, Lizzie lived in China, in a city called Hangchow. It is built over lagoons. There are many large harbours, and waterways everywhere, and twelve thousand stone bridges, some high enough for the tall-masted trading ships to sail beneath. It is a hundred miles all around the city, and untold thousands of citizens dwell there. It has twelve great gates, and palaces, temples, and gardens, all richer and finer than anything we have here.

In Hangchow the people wear silk and jewels, and drink wines made of rice and spices. The ladies are the most beauteous in the world, it is said. They ride in embroidered litters and wear jade pins in their hair, and marvellously jewelled headdresses.

Lizzie lived in a house by a canal, so her father could sell his jade to the merchants on the ships that sailed in. From all over the world they came. Her house had gardens and woods, silken pavilions hanging like tents by silver cords, and stables with many white horses, for her father was a great hunter. She told me she remembers pine trees in the snow, and hunting with a hawk, and riding with her father on his horse. And she remembers her mother sitting near a paper window, painting flowers on silk.

Then one day the sickness came, and many people died. Even Lizzie's family was not spared, and two of her brothers and her sister were taken. People were dying every day. There was no stopping the sickness; it was passed on words, on food, on breath, on hands. Nothing could stop the sickness from spreading.

In the end there were, in her family, only five left: her mother and father, her grandmother, one brother, and Lizzie herself. For years her father had talked of buying a ship and sailing to foreign lands to sell his jade. Also, during his talk with traders, he had befriended a merchant from England, who had invited him to visit him one day, if he should ever sail to that far land. Lizzie's father decided that now was the time to fulfil his ambitions. So he bought a ship and hired men to sail it to England. He brought Lizzie and her grandmother, mother, and brother away to this country. They brought, as well, many friends—several families—and relatives.

There was a storm when they neared land, and the ship broke up on rocks. Lizzie and her mother were in the sea, holding on to a big wooden box. It had all their family's belongings in it. Of that time, she remembers only the cold, and water all around, and darkness. She woke in sand with rain beating down upon her, and her mother's arms about her. There were some other people with them, but no one from their family. When daylight came, Lizzie saw the ship broke up on rocks, and the sands about strewn with bits of wood, boxes, shoes, and clothes. In one place was a long row of people, all dead.

Later came some folk who said they were Gypsies. They lived in little houses on wheels, pulled by horses. They were very kind, and looked after Lizzie and her mother and the others who had survived. After a time the other Chinese people left the Gypsies, saying they were going to build a new place for themselves. But Lizzie's mother was very sick and weak, so the two of them stayed with the Gypsies. Lizzie forgets how many summers they stayed—three or four, perhaps—though not all were spent in the same place, for the Gypsies were ever roving about.

It was a happy time, Lizzie says. They taught her to speak English words, and gave her her new name of Lizzie, and pulled her around on a little cart with wheels. Her mother wanted to go and find their own people, but couldn't walk far. Everywhere they went with the Gypsies, her mother asked if anyone had seen any Chinese people. The mother didn't like Gypsy ways. She called the Gypsies peasants and wouldn't learn their language, even though they were very kind. Lizzie's mother often told her tales of their home in China. She took dark silk thread and made Lizzie's Chinese name upon the red wedding-dress, so Lizzie would not forget. That dress was the most precious thing she had. It was the only thing they had from China; that, and Lizzie's little shoes. Everything else in the box was ruined by the sea.

One winter the mother's sickness got worse, and she coughed until she spat blood. An old Gypsy woman gave her medicines, but they didn't work, and she died.

For a few more seasons Lizzie stayed with the Gypsies. Then they all went to a village fair to sell medicines and jewellery the Gypsies had made, and Tybalt saw Lizzie. He wanted to buy her, but her new Gypsy mother wouldn't let him. That night one of the men took her to Tybalt, and sold her for a lot of money.

Tybalt hid her in a long box with swords wrapped in skins, and said that if she screamed or moved, the blades would cut out her tongue. So she stayed very still, though the next day she heard men and women shouting, and people screaming, and wagons being broke. They left then, and travelled a long time without stopping. Lizzie was much afraid.

In those early days she lived with Tybalt's family. She hated being with them. Math, Tybalt's second son, hounded her something merciless. When he wasn't tormenting her, he made her do his chores. His parents tried to stop him, but that made him worse; he teased her behind their backs, hit her where the bruises wouldn't show. At night she crawled away, but Tybalt always found her. Once he chased her with dogs. In the end he kept her in a cage. It was for her own protection, he said. It was better for business, too, he said, because people would think she was half animal, and a better freak for that.

For a summer and a winter she lived in that cage, until I came. After that, she said, all her life was changed.

And the rest of her story you will come to know, Brother Benedict, for it is woven close with mine.

SEVEN

OOD DAY, BROTHER! I see Jing-wei's story got you all inspired yesterday, and you've drawn Tybalt's sword at the end of the narrative! A fine book you'll make, if you carry on with your excellent illustration—splendid almost as the books in your great library.

Now, to my tale again:

That summer with Tybalt wore on, beaten by the heat into languid hours of laziness and boredom. Even the river was sluggish and warm, and the children, playing in it, were barely refreshed. Dogs lay panting in the shade, and I reckoned even the birds were swooning in the heat, for we seldom heard their songs. In the cool of early morn Richard hunted deer for us, and we caught fish from the river. We took great care of our fires, that they did not spread in the parched woods. In the evenings we ate bread and cold meat, and tried to keep the children quiet. Several times Richard entertained them with his father's sword. He used it as Tybalt had, twirling the blade fast about himself, and slicing off the tips of twigs that the children held out in their hands. I confess I was envious; he was the way I wished to be, graceful and strong, with the power to make maids' eyes shine. Once he gave me the sword and told me to do a trick or two with it. He was mocking me, as usual, for he knew I could barely lift the thing; but I swung it about a little, thinking of that happy hour when I had held it in Tybalt's pavilion, as entertainment for the folk of Rokeby. As I handed it back to him, Richard said, "This sword shall slay another dragon one day."

"Are you a seer now?" I asked.

"Nay, not me," he said, "but I met an old woman once who was a soothsayer. It was five summers past, but I have not forgot. She foretold a plague of fires that would herald the coming of another dragon, the last of them all. And she said this sword would kill the beast. One of her prophecies has come true."

His eyes wore a strange gleam, and I got away as quick as I could, thinking he was mad.

One day soon after, we smelled smoke, and the sweltering skies turned hazy bronze. Tybalt went riding out with several men to see the cause of the fire, and came back saying it was far on the other side of the river, and seeming to rise from one place. "'Tis no small village this time," he said. "This time it's a large town."

"It weren't the Scots, then, playing games," said a woman. "They'd not take on a town."

Tybalt shook his head and looked very grave, but said no more. We stayed where we were, and were quiet, and lit as few fires as possible.

One afternoon a lone horsemen came. We were all afeared it

was the lord who owned the land we were on, and that Richard would hang for poaching his game; but it was a travelling minstrel, and he stayed with us the evening, and broke the jaded hours with thrilling songs. He also had stories that disturbed: accounts of towns and villages and harvest fields turned utterly to ash. These he had seen with his own eyes. People were fleeing to the hills to hide, he said, or else digging burrows in the earth, or making boathouses for themselves in marshy land, which would not burn.

"We know, now, what is the cause of it," he said, and I held my breath. "There have been several accounts of a winged beast. Then there was a sighting by twenty sailors all at once, and every man swore on holy writ that what he said was true. I know; I was in the port when they told it to the priests. They told of a beach on the western coast, with rugged cliffs and sands of greyish white, like ash. It was sunset when they sailed past, and they saw, flying low along the shore, a beast with wings. While they watched they saw it rise up and disappear into a cave in the cliff. It is St. Alfric's Cove, they said, for there is a little shrine there where once the saint had been shipwrecked, and was led ashore by seals. He lived there, a hermit, for more than fifty winters, eating fish the seals brought him."

"There must have been a dragon egg missed during the great searches," said Tybalt, his face grave. We were sitting around a single fire, for the children had gone to bed, and we were picking the last of the bones and drinking ale. "My father said dragons are fifty years in the shell, and the young beasts are fledglings a dozen years or more, afore they can fly any distance. There must have been just one egg that survived. Perchance even more."

"There is only one dragon," said the minstrel. "All accounts are the same: all tell of a winged beast with a tail bent partway along, as if it did not form properly in the egg. 'Tis red-gold, so they say, and huge, with a neck as long as a tower, and wings like a ship's sails, and teeth like plough blades. Myself, I doubt the size; the dragons of old were generally small, though no less deadly for that."

I looked at Richard. He was staring into the flames, his head bent, but I saw the glitter of his eyes, and could guess his thought.

"Could a lone beast burn a whole village?" a woman asked.

The minstrel picked up a handful of dust, letting it trickle through his fingers in the firelight like golden sand. "In the heat that plagues these present days," he replied, "a burning straw could set a whole city alight. The land is tinder dry. And if the summer goes on like this, and a dragon is about, then it has the power to burn half the kingdom."

"But our good king will send his finest soldiers to kill it, for sure," said someone else. "Mayhap they're on their way, as we speak."

"Alas, there's no such plot," said the minstrel. "The king is busy at war with the French and the Scots, and has more than enough to worry on. The dragon won't be crushed until after the wars. Not unless there's a mighty hunter among us ordinary folk, with the courage and cunning to slay the beast."

Gloom fell on us all, but I saw Richard's face lit up by the flames, transfixed and radiant, as if he heard a summons.

"Where is St. Alfric's Cove?" Richard asked. "Near what town?"

"'Tis about two days' walk beyond the city of Twells," said the minstrel, "through the villages of Crick and Seagrief. Seagrief itself is on the edge of the cliff overlooking St. Alfric's Cove, and the folk there keep a fire burning every night, to warn ships away from the rocks. 'Tis a remote place, not often visited."

Talk turned to other things. Soon after, I went to bed, curled up under Tybalt's wagon, and I was glad that Richard went on watch again. My dreams that night were terrible.

The next day the heat was worse. Not a breath stirred the leaves or the dust, and the air was taut as a bowstring just afore the arrow is released. Tybalt said he smelled a storm, so one of the lads climbed a tree and looked beyond the woods, and spied black clouds brewing on the edge of the world.

The air grew tenser still, and even breathing parched my throat. All our nerves were overstretched, for there were several fights, mothers were sharp-tongued with their children, and the dogs were snappish. Everything shimmered in the heat, and the floor of Lizzie's cage was too hot to touch. I took her buckets of water, and she tipped them slowly over herself and became cleaner than ever, as well as cool awhile. I begged a spare dress from one of the women, and Lizzie changed from her grey rags to a chestnut-coloured garment that suited her well, though it was too big. Then, herself content, she craved me to look after the bear and cat as well. One of the younger lads had the task of tending them, but he was lazy about it, and I suppose the beasts were suffering. The bear, especially, was in bad shape. It would not drink, even when I risked life and limb, for Lizzie's sake, and reached through the bars of its cage with a cup and poured water onto its lolling tongue. It did not move. There were maggots in its eyes and lips, and its mangy fur crawled with lice.

"It's dying, I think," I said to Tybalt.

"Aye," he agreed, when he had been to inspect it. "It will be better killed, and we'll eat its meat."

Lizzie was sorely upset when I told her. "It will be better for it to be killed today, Lizzie," I told her, "for 'tis suffering something terrible in this heat, and otherwise will die slowly, of starvation and thirst."

The lads cheered when Tybalt said the bear would be used for food that night, for they were all wrought up and in fine fettle for some fun. Led by Richard, and with much crowing and laughing, they tied ropes about the bear's neck and dragged it from the cage. It hardly fought, it was already so far gone. They tied it up between two trees, and set the dogs on it. I've seen bearbaiting before and never liked it much; but this, with a bear helpless and sick, was hard to look upon, and I wondered that Tybalt allowed it.

Seeing the bear suffer so drove Lizzie from her wits. She howled worse than the bear, and threw herself against the side of her cage as if she would break herself free to rescue it. By the time I opened her door and pulled her from the bars, her brow and arms were bruised. Like a fiend she fought, cursing and screaming in her own language. Suddenly she went limp against me, sobbing as if her heart would break. At last the bear was dead, and she grew quiet. I sat with her on the cage floor and held her while she wept, stroking her hair the way I had, in times past, comforted Addy or the twins when they were woebegone.

While we sat that way a shadow passed overhead, and black clouds covered up the sun. The heat eased a little, and thunder rolled. I looked up and saw Richard watching us. He had a fever-ish look these days, as if a secret, huge and mad, consumed him. Now malice and scorn were added to the frenzy, and it worried me.

Soon after, while I was alone down by the river washing Lizzie's food bowl, he came and stood beside me and said, very soft, "She's a comely maid, when she's polished up."

I said nothing, for I smelled evil on its way.

"You must be letching for her, Jude," he went on.

"And you must be daft," said I.

"Come on, I've seen the way you are with her! 'Tis nought to be shameful of. You've had a maid before, haven't you?"

"Aye." I bent over the bowl, scouring it again with sand, though it was already clean.

He crouched down by me, and I could feel him looking at my face, laughing. "Liar, Jude of Doran. But Lizzie—well, there's a maid for your first! Hapless and helpless, and right grateful to you. She'd need no persuading."

I stood up to walk away, but he gripped my sleeve. Smiling, he was full of villainy. "If you won't take her, Jude, I may be tempted to myself. I've a mind to have a maid, afore I face hell."

The bit about hell I didn't understand, but the rest of it was clear. A kind of rage befell me, and I lifted Lizzie's metal bowl and banged it down hard on the top of Richard's head. He didn't fall, but he looked mighty surprised, then he hit me in the stom-ach. I collapsed like a puppet, and lay curled on the dirt while he kicked me. People came to watch, some telling him to stop, others laughing and saying that, for all his size, Jude of Doran was a right milksop. At last someone stopped Richard, and I was left alone to recover. I bled and spewed a bit, then cleaned myself up in the river, collected Lizzie's bowl, and staggered back to her cage. She said nothing at first, until I handed her the bowl, and she saw the dent in it. Then she said, straight-faced as a nun: "'Tis a pity you had not gone down to empty my privy bucket, Jude. It would have fit over his head nicely, and not been dented."

"Richard isn't worth a turd," I said, and she laughed. I laughed with her, and it was good, that mirth, for it eased the hurt in both of us. And while we laughed the storm broke and rain began to fall, heavy and hard. I locked her cage door—a small act I had grown to loathe—and pulled the cover across. One corner I left folded up, so she could watch the children dancing in the downpour.

Everyone went mad in that thunderstorm. By God's soul, it was a blessed relief! I stood out in it, face upturned and washed of dust, cool water on my tongue and throat, and all of me baptised with rain.

All evening it rained, and I went to bed in Tybalt's wagon, with his family, since the ground outside was running mud. Richard said he would go on watch that night, though his father said there was no need. "A dragon wouldn't see past its own smoke, in this storm," Tybalt said, but Richard got his knife and bow anyway, and a heavy cloak, and went out into the teeming dark.

At some time in the night I woke, and for one blessed moment thought I was at home again, with my family breathing all around. But the rain, instead of landing quiet on the thatch, was drumming on a wooden roof; and that made me remember, and the pain crushed down on me again. I slept, and had a dream that Richard came inside and bent over me to strangle me. I woke sweating and hot, and needing to let out some of the evening's ale. Quiet, I pulled on my boots and went outside.

All was hushed, for the rain had passed and a full moon sailed, ship-like, between the rolling clouds. I went down to the river, and on my way back looked over to Lizzie's cage. The cover had been pulled off, though I could see little else in the shadows beneath the trees. My hand reached for her key tied to my belt. It was not there. The leather thong was sliced through, smooth and neat, as with a knife. So it was no dream I had, of Richard! He had been there right enough, but thieving instead of throttling.

I ran then, slithering in the mud, and found Lizzie's cage empty, the door open. I wanted to call her, but I dared not. What if she wanted to go with him? Mayhap they often stole away together, and I would but make a fool of myself by following. In an agony of doubt I stood listening, but could hear only the thumping of my own heart. Then a call. Shrill and afraid; a maid's voice.

'Twas all I needed. I went into the trees, towards the sound. It was pitch-black in the shadows under the trees, though in parts the moonbeams poured through, bright almost as the day. Water dripped all around, and my feet squelching in the mud must have been heard a mile away. By corpus bones, I was afraid! Afraid of finding them, and afraid of not finding them. And if they were found, what would I do? Never would I beat Richard in a fight. I stopped, thinking to go back and call Tybalt. But would he laugh, and tell me to leave his son to his wenching? If he cared nothing for the sufferings of the bear, why should he care for Lizzie?

Hardly breathing for terror, and wishing I had brought my bow, I went deeper into the woods. I stumbled on a root and fell heavily, sliding some way in the mud, and making more noise than a pig in a panic. As I got to my feet I had half a mind to go back anyway, and trust to fate that Lizzie was willing with him. At that moment I heard a voice, muffled and low, and full of threat. Richard's voice. But no sound from Lizzie. Quiet, I crept forward. I could see nothing in the shadows, but I heard Richard speak again. Of a sudden I noticed, in a pool of moonlight on the muddy ground, a patch of scarlet, dark as blood. I picked it up; it was Lizzie's silken dress, that I had washed. I looked up, peering through the dark. And then I saw them, two blacker shapes against the darkness of a tree. Lizzie stood against the trunk, and he was pressed against her. Uncertainty flooded over me again. If she were unwilling, would she not call out? I dropped the dress and was about to creep away; but then I saw a flash of steel near Lizzie's throat. Without thought I rushed at Richard to haul him off. Hearing me, he swung around, the knife still in his hand. I saw his teeth glimmer as if he laughed, and he slashed towards me so quick, I heard the whistle of the blade. Somehow it missed, and I stepped backwards and fell. Then he was on me, and I was holding his arm with the knife, but the point was cruelly close to my face. His other arm pressed across my throat, so hard that I could not breathe, and for an age all was suffocating pain and fear; then I saw stars and fire, and thought the dragon and death and hell had come.

Then of a sudden the weight across my throat was gone, though something heavy fell across the rest of me; and I drew in breath at last. It was Richard across me, limp as a sack of flour. I threw him off and got to my feet. Lizzie was close, a stump of wood in her hands. In the moonlight her face was parchment white, and her eyes shimmered and were full of fear. She dropped the wood and backed away, wiping her hands on her skirts as if to clean them.

"Sweet Jesus—I've killed him!" she said.

I bent down and put my hand upon Richard's chest. All seemed deadly still. Blood matted his hair above his right ear, and ran from his nose. I dared not put my hand upon his parted lips, to see if there was breath. Standing, I asked Lizzie if she was harmed. She shook her head, then spied her silken dress, and hobbled across the muddy ground to pick it up.

"He told me he was setting me free," she said. "That's why I brought my mother's dress, and wore my shoes. He said you had given him the key to my cage, and would be waiting for me, to take me away. He said I would never live in the cage again. His words were sweet, and he was kind. That's why I came quietly with him. And then, when we were here, afar off in the trees . . ."

"I'd made no plot with him," I said. "He cut your key from my belt while I slept. But I woke after, saw your cage open, and came to look for you."

At that moment we heard a shout and the barking of dogs. I looked towards our camp, but could see nothing. Had Tybalt found her cage unlocked, and thought she had escaped? God's soul, there'd be a hunt now, for sure, and blame laid somewhere! And as for Richard, lying like a corpse—

"They'll hang me for murder!" whispered Lizzie, looking at

him. Richard groaned just then, and moved a little. Dogs barked and howled, coming nearer.

Without thought, I swept Lizzie up into my arms and ran. And as I ran clouds covered up the moon again and rain began to fall, and I remember thanking God, for it meant my footsteps would be lost in mud, and no one could hunt us down.

Like a nightmare it was, that flight. I could see nothing for the darkness and the rain, and though Lizzie was a little thing, she was heavy after hours of carrying, with the wetness in our clothes weighing us both down, and the mud ankle deep at times. Sometimes I could have sworn I saw wolves' eyes shining at us through the rain, and once we heard something huge—a bear, possibly—crashing through the woods alongside of us. We stumbled into trees and rolled down banks, and a hundred times I slipped and fell, hurting us both, and all the while we were driven on by the dogs howling like fiends in hell.

And on that fiendish note I think I shall end for today, Brother Benedict. I hear the bells tolling for prayers—a peaceful note, after my tale's terror. What? You want me to go on? Well, it is tempting to, and such kindly devotion to your task is most commendable; but I did plight my word to the Abbot that I would never keep you from your prayers. So off with you! Godspeed! I swear I shall not start again without you.

EIGHT

 REETINGS, BROTHER! You are ready early today, your quill neatly sharpened, I see, and candles already lit, and a merry fire in the grate. A good day for writing, this, with rain outside and a cold autumn wind a-blowing! You have the better task, I think: I just saw Brother Nicholas out in the yard trying to round up the geese and head them into the barn. The Abbot wants their feathers kept in fine fettle, since they're his only supply of quills. He's very determined to have a pile of books copied out, so he can begin his dream of teaching every soul to read. I'm not sure that the geese will be right thrilled about it; they've few enough tail feathers already.

All right, I'll continue! God's truth, you monks have lively ways of getting across your wants, despite your vows of silence!

I did not rest that night. I followed the river upstream, knowing it would take us from the woods and back to the town. A little after cockcrow we left the trees, to find a sunny day. I was mortal weary but dared not stop, knowing Tybalt valued Lizzie and would likely be out on his horse, searching. But I changed the way of carrying Lizzie, and took her on my back, as I oft had carried little Addy. It was easier that way, and Lizzie could hold on with her arms about my neck. Travelling northwestwards, we avoided the town, skirting the tilled fields and the meadows, then kept to the tracks through the moorlands. We passed villages and farms, and saw people shearing sheep while others washed the fleeces in the streams. I thought of my mother twisting yarn upon her distaff, and my heart ached. All of me ached, from memories and weariness, and from the beating Richard had given me the day before.

Near the middle of the day I stopped to rest. We had been walking through stony moors following a stream, which I supposed would lead to villages further ahead, where we might get food and shelter for the night. We stopped by an old oak tree, and I set Lizzie down in the shade. "I need to sleep," I said. "I can't walk night and day without rest."

Crouching by the water, I drank deeply. It was brackish but quenching. Lizzie crouched nearby to drink.

"Would you like a swim?" I asked, thinking of the day I had danced in the river with her and raised Tybalt's ire.

"I think not," she said. I was sorry, for I would gladly have carried her in again.

When we had finished drinking she got her mother's silken dress from where she had dropped it on the grass, and washed it in the shallows, cleaning off the grime from last night in the woods. I offered to help her, but she shook her head and went on with the washing, dipping the scarlet folds in the stream, then rubbing them carefully to get off the stains. I wondered that she held the silk so dear, then remembered it was all she had of her old life, all she had of her family. And I thought how I would have given much to have just one little thing my parents had owned, some tiny link, something I could touch that was of them.

The washing done, she limped up to the tree and hung the silk across a branch to dry. Then she stood at the edge of the shade, looking out across the rolling wastes we had crossed. Very still she stood, her eyes like polished ebony, her gold-brown skin as glowing as the day. I had not often seen her on her feet, for she had been always sitting in her cage, or else lying on the ground while I cleaned it out; and it was odd to see her standing free like that, beside the wild moors. Looking at her, I felt awkward of a sudden, for her skirts were wet and clinging, and she was willow-slender and graceful, and pleasing to the eye.

Limping back, she came and sat at my feet, close, her arms about her knees, her gaze still on the moors. "Do you think Tybalt will find us?" she asked.

"He'll not find us now," I said. "The rain has washed away our tracks, and his dogs will never get the smell of us."

"If Richard dies, what then? Will they look again for us, and hang me on a gallows?"

"Nay. Richard won't die. 'Twill take more than a chip of wood to kill him off—'twill take a falling oak."

She laughed a little. "What will we do, Jude?"

"Find a village and beg some food and a place by a fire tonight. On the morrow we'll seek a place for you to stay. A nunnery, mayhap, where you'll be looked after."

Frowning, she asked, "What will you do?"

"Find a farmer to hire me for work. The lords pay people well to have their land tilled these days, since the Black Death killed off so many of their workers. I heard that some of the larger estates are going to ruin, from want of men to work them."

"I could work on a farm."

"I think not, Lizzie. Maids either marry or they become nuns. Unless they're highborn, and then they might live in lord's houses, and serve the ladies there."

"I'm highborn."

"That's different."

"Why?"

"Our highborn maids are not made lame."

"Then there's no place for me."

"I didn't say that. I think a nunnery would be best. It doesn't mean you have to be a nun; the nuns would look after you until you found something else to do. It would not be an unpleasant life."

"How do you know? Have you lived in a nunnery?"

"No. But it would be better than a cage, I'll warrant."

"It would be a different kind of cage. I don't want to live in a nunnery."

"By God's soul, Lizzie, give me peace! I don't want to discuss this now! I've walked all night and half today, and I'm bone weary. I'm tired of fretting about my own fate, let alone yours. Let me sleep for now, and we'll talk on this later."

I lay down in the shade. Lizzie didn't move, but she made a little sound as if she wept, and I was sorry I had spoken sharp with her. Remorseful, too tired to make amends, I put my arm across my eyes and tried to sleep. But although it was pleasant there by the stream, and I was weary to the bones, I found I could not rest. My nerves were jangled, and a worm gnawed at my conscience, over Richard, and because I had stole a maid well paid for by her owner. Also, as the full import of what I'd done began to dawn on me, there were other worries.

I'd had little to do with a maid before, apart from my sisters and the taunting Prue. How would it be between Lizzie and me, now that we were fugitives and wayfarers together? What would people think of us, her plainly not my kin, nor I her husband? How would we sleep together in the fields? Close for safety, or decently separate? And what of all the ordinary things I would normally do in private—like picking my teeth or my nose, or scratching myself, or farting, or moving my bowels? 'Tis all very well for you to laugh, Brother Benedict, but all these things were mortal worrying to me, at the time. I even felt discomforted trying to sleep that afternoon, knowing Lizzie sat nearby, mayhap watching me. It is one thing to feed and tend for a maid in a prison, another to live with her in liberty.

I slept at last. When I awoke, the sun was on its downward journey, and Lizzie was gone, the red dress with her. Alarmed, I leaped to my feet, thinking Tybalt had come and snatched her off. But then I spied her stumbling and limping further on, still following the stream.

Cursing, I ran after her. I got to her at last, and grabbed her arm. Her face was wet with tears and sweat, and she must have been in agony from walking all that way.

"What are you doing, dimwit?" I asked.

"I'm going on alone," she said, trying to walk on, sobbing

with every step. Her shoes and bandages were red.

"Why alone?" I asked.

"Because I won't be a nun. And I won't be a millstone around your neck, neither. You have no duty to help me out."

"Oh, Lizzie, 'tis not from duty!" I said.

"What is it, then? Do you think on me as Richard did?"

"No! Never that!" Taking both her shoulders, I made her stop. She stood with her arms crossed over her mother's dress, her eyes downcast. She looked so small, so all undone, that I near wept myself, from pity.

"Truth to tell, Lizzie," I said, "you remind me of my sister Addy. More, I have no home, no family, and I feel . . . well, I feel akin with you. It helps me to help you, for it gives me a reason to live. I'll not put you in a nunnery, nor make you do anything you are against, I swear. Now, can we travel on together, in peace?"

She smiled a little, and climbed onto my back again, and we went on. The stream was a good guide, for it kept us watered, and took us to more fields of yellow wheat ripe for harvest, then to a village. We spied some fresh-baked oaten cakes cooling in a window, and I'm ashamed to confess that I stole them, for we were hungry.

I felt stronger after we had eaten, and walked more quickly, following the lane out of the village, still heading west, my eyes lowered against the sinking sun. I had no idea where I was, or what villages we passed, since I could not read the milestones on the roads. I thought only to put as many miles as I could betwixt ourselves and Tybalt. Sometimes on the lanes between the villages we passed other wayfarers, all travelling on foot: pilgrims on their way home after visiting shrines, or black-gowned friars, or peddlers with pots and pans, charcoal sellers, traders, and lepers. But by sunset the tracks and lanes were deserted, and I began to be haunted by fears of demons and ghosts. And I remembered that the dragon was said to fly at dusk and dawn, and now was a devilishly dangerous time to be out. I wished I had looked sooner for a house to stay.

There was a village near, for I could see its church tower above the trees. I cut across a meadow full of rye, and came to the tiny hamlet just as the sun went down. It was a village such as Doran had been, too small for an inn, with only a square-towered Norman church and a few thatch-and-mud houses crouched either side of the dirt lane. Behind the houses I could just make out, in the gathering gloom, the crofts with summer vegetables well grown, and tiny farm buildings, and a cart and plough or two. I stood Lizzie on her feet and she waited in the darkling lane as I approached a house.

Firelight glowed inside and smoke came out the windows, smelling of beans and vegetable broth. From within came sounds of running feet, children shrieking with laughter, boys quarrelling, and a dog barking. Above it all a baby bawled lustily, and a woman shouted for peace. I banged on the door, and there was instant silence inside.

"You'd best open it, Edwin," said the woman's voice. "Well, go on! You're the man of the house now."

There was the sound of a bolt cautiously drawn back, and the door opened a crack. I glimpsed part of a face and one wary eye, before the door was slammed shut again. "It do be a maid and a lad, Ma," said a lad.

"Well, don't stand there pop-eyed, let them in."

The door was opened wide, and I went back to Lizzie, and she leaned on me as we entered in. The lad who admitted us stood on the threshold a moment, scanning the evening skies; then he banged the door shut and bolted it again.

For long moments there was total quiet, but for the yelping of a small dog as it jumped around Lizzie and me. Little could I see, for smoke, but the boy threw a bundle of wood on the fire, and in the leaping flame-light I saw three little children go and cling to their mother's skirt. Their eyes, as round as plates, were fixed on Lizzie's face. Two other children moved closer to a boy of about ten summers, who crouched on the dirt by the fire and stirred a cauldron of broth. Pigs and poultry roamed in the rushes on the floor, and a cow with large curving horns was tethered in one corner. The smells, the homeliness, awoke a deep longing in me.

"You've brought the freak," said the woman, holding her babe closer, and making the sign of the cross. "The freak from the fair. Like Old Lan. God help us all."

"Her name's Lizzie," I said. "I beg of you, good mother, let us stay. And give us, if you will, a bite of food each, and we'll be gone by morning. We'll not harm you or rob you, I swear by Jesus' blessed tree."

"It's not robbing I'm worried on," she said, jiggling the babe to keep it quiet. "The freak's an evil maid, a heathen. I'll not have her in this house. Nor you. It's not right, you travelling alone with her. I'll thank you to leave, and right quick."

I began to plead with her, but the eldest boy edged past us and opened the door again, and began to push me out. Lizzie clung to my sleeve, and I was still begging for a bed for the night, when the woman started to scream.

"Out! Out!" she shrieked. "Out, afore I call the priest to chase you out, and your devils with you! Out!"

I picked Lizzie up and backed out into the night. Still the woman yelled, and people began to come out of the other houses. Hearing the woman's shouts, and doubtless thinking we were thieves, they all started screaming, and some threw stones. One hit Lizzie, making her cry out. A man came out and set his hound on us. I ran then, raising dust in the shadowy lane, while people shouted and cursed, and stones rained all around, and the hound snapped and snarled at my heels. I don't know how far I ran, trying to get away from the damned thing, while Lizzie nearly choked me with her arms, and I shook all over from terror and fatigue. We left the dog at last, and I stumbled on down the pitch-black road. A silver moon was rising, and I could see wheat on either side, and trees black against the starry sky, but little else. Then somewhere in the fields a wolf howled, and I glimpsed yellow eyes in the darkness to my left, and was sure a pack was after me. I started running again, gasping and blind, half choked by Lizzie's arms about my neck. Then something flew out of the wheat beside the lane, its wings whirring in the quiet dark, and I near lost my wits from fright. I ran again, and tripped and fell. I remember that, as I went down, I tried to turn so I would not fall on Lizzie. There was a sharp pain in my foot, and I suppose I smashed my head upon a stone, for all became bright stars and blackness, and that is the last thing I remember of that night.

And that, I think, is enough to write for now. It must be almost time for bells, Brother, and a mug of mead.

NINE

 TRAIGHT TO OUR TALE today, and no meander-
ing! It was daylight when I came to. My left foot
burned and ached, and my head throbbed as if it
were being hammered by a fiend. I opened my
eyes and saw a brilliant light shaped like a man, and thought it
was an angel. I closed my eyes and dreamed that I had died and
St. Peter was stabbing his finger at my skull, trying to knock
some sense into me. When I opened my eyes again I saw that it
was not an angel before me, but a silver robe. And later still, I
saw that I was in a room with sunlight pouring in the door and
falling on a soldier's armour that hung on a hook. And beside me
was an old woman, brown and shrivelled as a nut, with wispy
white hair pulled back in a knot, and white whiskers on her chin.
And her black eyes, half lost beneath the wrinkles, were the
same shape as Lizzie's eyes.

"Sweet Jesus save me," I said. "I've died and gone to Lizzie's
heaven."

The old woman cackled like a hen, and I saw she had but two yellow teeth. "By all the powers, 'tis no heaven!" she said. Then, looking behind her, she called, "Come and see him, child. The boy's awake."

I looked beyond the woman's shoulder and saw a doorway with bright sunlight shining through. And through that light came Lizzie, transfigured, wearing a dress of crimson and green, and with her hair brushed and braided smooth as ravens' wings. Right lovely she was. And she was walking, wearing ordinary shoes, though small ones.

"I have died," I said, and fainted again.

Then someone was pouring cool water onto my tongue, and washing my hot face. After a time I woke fully, and began to look about me. I was lying on a pile of straw, a blanket over me. Between my bed and the open door crouched the old woman, lighting a fire in the middle of the floor. The air was still and hot, and the blue smoke rose about her, ascending to the rafters where hung sacks of grain, beside two pigs and several fish on hooks, smoking. There were bunches of herbs hanging on the walls, and strings of onions and garlic. My eyes travelled around the walls, and I saw more clearly the mail armour on its hook, with its helmet nearby in a little alcove, and a great sword shining across two pegs above. There were shelves too numerous for me to number, laden with freakish things. Through the smoke's blue veil I made out jars of feathers and claws and oddly shaped sticks, shadowy carvings, and whitish objects that might have been bone. There were wizened roots, glowing stones, carven boxes such as I had never seen before, and other things, foreign and mysterious, I could not name. And in the sun on the step, and at the foot of my straw bed, were two cats, both black as coal.

The old woman came over to me, lifted the blanket at my feet, and pressed something hard against my sore ankle. I tried to pull away, but she was strong, for all her littleness.

"'Tis an arrowhead, boy," she said. "'Twill ease the swelling, and your pain." Then she sang a charm: "Come out, worm—out from the marrow into the bone, from the bone into the flesh, from the flesh into the skin, from the skin into this arrow."

I whispered amen, to cover the spell with the Church's blessing, just in case.

No need to snort like that, Brother, nor to frown so disapprovingly. I know what you are thinking, and that you must blame me for staying in that house. But I had no choice about it. When I asked Lizzie later how I came to be there, she said that when I had fallen in the lane she saw firelight in a house, and went to it. I suppose the flickering flames were what I had mistook for wolves' eyes. Anyway, the old woman came out to the lane with Lizzie and together they dragged me to the house. Once there I could not move for the pain in my head, nor could I have walked for the soreness in my ankle, and I was forced by fate to stay for good or ill. And that's the naked truth, as God is God.

The crone was called Old Lan. She was Chinese, the same as Lizzie, and she too had had bound feet. Hers she had straightened, and could walk almost normally, except that she hobbled with age. She must have been near ninety, but from what I could tell, there was nothing wrong with her hearing or her sight, and her mind was sharp as a knife. She was a scold, too, and I soon learned not to argue with her, even when she poured her nasty potions down my throat. She dosed me up right well, in those early days, and I have to say that her concoctions gave great ease. My ankle, that I had twisted bad, she mended with the arrow. I had a bad cut on my head, which she put cobwebs on and healed.

Brother Benedict, will you please stop doing that? I've confessed all this to the Abbot, and he's shriven me, and said a blessing over me. Now can we get on with the tale? I'd like to think I can tell it truly, as it happened, without you frowning and tut-tutting and splattering ink every time you cross yourself.

Now, I'll tell you of my life those days, in Old Lan's house. At first I was as restricted as Lizzie in my walks, because of my sore ankle, and so I stayed mainly about the dwelling, resting in the shade. Lizzie went on short walks with Lan, or helped in the garden, or they sat on stones under the trees, talking together for hours like old acquaintances. When working in the house, Lizzie sat upon a stool to spare her feet, and she seemed at home, content with her lot.

I cannot say I shared her contentment. I feared Old Lan, and sorely resented the fates that made me stay. Though Lan had commanded me to stay abed and rest, whenever she was out of the house I got up and stood on my hurt foot, hoping to strengthen it, thus hastening the day when Lizzie and I might leave.

One afternoon, while Lan and Lizzie were out in the garden, I hopped over to the suit of armour, to inspect it. It was dusty and dull with smoke, but beautifully made, each link in the mail skilfully joined. I lifted it in my hand; it was heavy, but slid and moved like a silver skin. Leaving it, I lifted the sword from the wall, withdrawing it from its steel scabbard. It was heavier than Tybalt's sword and cunningly etched with wondrous designs. There were jewels about the handle, and a coat of arms in scarlet and blue. I wondered who the man was who had owned it, and how it came to be here in Lan's house, with the armour and helmet. What was his name, and who had been his lord?

"His name was Ambrose," Lan said, coming inside, her arms full of vegetables. "He was a knight, sorely wounded, and stayed here for healing. I told you to rest your foot, boy. I know you're eager to be gone, but you don't hasten healing, walking before you should."

I put the sword away, unnerved because she knew my thoughts. It was one of her less alarming habits, knowing what lay in people's heads—and in their hearts, no doubt.

Lizzie came in, too, her hands dusty with the soil, and with dirt smudged across her cheek. She smiled at me across Lan's bent back, then sat on the dirt floor in the shade. Both cats leaped from the hearth and curled up in Lizzie's lap. They were like fond kittens with her, though they snarled and spat at me. Lan crouched by her fire and began cutting up a cabbage and throwing it into the broth.

"You knew this knight well, old mother?" Lizzie asked.

Lan put down the knife and rested back on her heels, her eyes peering through the smoke, beyond it, to things I could not see. I sat on the bed, sensing a story brewing.

"Aye, I knew him well," Lan replied, soft and dream-like. "He was manly and tall, and lithe as a whip, once his scars were healed. Beautiful he was; my joy, and the love of my life. And I was the love of his."

I smiled, for she was mortal ugly. "I was a young widow then," she went on, "as comely as Jing-wei. I found him on the lane one day, much as I found you, Jude. He was covered with ash, and he could hardly stand nor speak from pain and weariness. I brought him here, and helped him take off his armour, so that he could lie down and sleep. And under the mail his tunic was scorched to rags, and in parts melted onto his skin, for he was sorely burned. And when I washed the dust and ash from his face, his skin came off as well. All over he was burned, and the scars were a long time healing.

"He had killed a dragon, though not before it breathed on him. Long had he studied the beasts, and knew much of their habits and weaknesses. He had a fine mind, did Ambrose, curious and well informed. He was right brave, and gentle, too. Never had I met a soul so tender, so full of loving gratitude for every day, so near to joy. He healed in time, though his skin remained scarred, even on his face, and one eye would never wholly open, nor close. He never went back to his lord, or to his lands. He stayed with me, and we loved. Then one day he sickened, and there were red lumps upon him, in his armpits and groin, and in his neck. By that night he was dead, and my heart's joy with him. I buried him under the apple tree, and every spring I gather the blossoms as they fall, and put them upon my bed, and sleep touched by his transfigured skin."

I thought the story morbid, and was glad the blossoming was done, and hoped there were no withered petals left where I lay at night. When I looked at Lizzie her face was wet with tears. She got up, spilling the cats into the sun on the step, limped over to Lan, and put her arms about her. They were like grandmother and grandchild, kinswomen, close and alike in soul. Seeing them together made me ache for my own kin, and I got up and hobbled outside. Afore I knew it, I was crying as well. I knew not why; but loneliness went through me like a sword, and with all my being I longed for kin to put their arms about me. And I was guilty. God's soul, I was guilty! Guilty for the way I had spoken to little Addy that last night, and refused to take her to Rokeby with me, thereby causing her death. Guilty because I had survived, when I should have died with them. Guilty because the thing that slew them still roamed free, and I did nothing about it. And so I bowed over in the grass and sobbed, stricken with remorse and pain, and not knowing how I could live.

After a time my grief was spent, and I pulled up handfuls of grass and wiped my face and nose, and tried to gather up my fortitude. I realised, of a sudden, that Lizzie was sitting on one side of me, and Lan on the other.

"Lord, I'm a fool!" I said.

"No fool around here," said Lan. "Just a boy a-sorrowing. My Ambrose, he could weep like that, too, and he did, oft times, for all his manliness. I knew he had left behind more than his lord and lands; that he had left a wife and children. He never spoke of them, but when they were in his heart there was fear, too, and he used to rub the scars upon his face, and weep. It was an unnecessary fear, for of all God's creatures he was the most beautiful."

"Would his wife have loved him, if he had gone back?" asked Lizzie.

"I never asked the fates," said Lan. "I took what they gave me, and was grateful. But I saw how his spirit was troubled because of what he had abandoned—not only his obligations as husband and father, but also his duty as a knight. And I knew that, no matter how great our joy together, he would never know true peace."

Then they both got up and went inside, for it was sunset, and supper was almost done.

And our supper must be near ready, Brother. I'll stop here, and take Jing-wei for a walk in the orchard, since the sun is out just now. Doubtless you'd like some spare time yourself, maybe to visit old Father Matthew. Jing-wei said he has taken a turn for the worse, and is dying now. I'm sorry; I know he was the abbot here before his wits left him, and that you're all passing fond of him. Jing-wei says he is never alone, and one of the brothers sits with him every moment, to keep him loving company on his last journey.

Well, I'll see you at supper. It'll be Brother Tom's bean soup again, no doubt—God have mercy on us all!

TEN

ORRY I'M A LITTLE LATE, Brother; I've been in the orchard again, helping bring in the apples, and storing them on their racks in the huge pantry. I worked with Brother Tobit, and he kept me well entertained with his tales and bawdy jokes. I love his wit: I notice he's the jester in the common room in the evenings, when you're all allowed to relax and talk, afore the hours of the night and the Great Silence. When we finished with the fruit he showed me the barn, fair bursting with straw and hay and grain. I marvelled that you monks could use it all, but he explained it's for guests as well. He said that often manor lords or ladies come, with hundreds of servants, soldiers, and all their horses and hounds besides, and you're duty-bound to give them hospitality, sometimes for weeks. Well, at least Jing-wei and I help out with the work, so I don't feel too bad eating your food, even if it is only Brother Tom's everlasting beans— Don't jab me with your pen! I'll get on with it!

Two things happened at Lan's house that changed the lives of Lizzie and me. The first was to do with Lizzie's feet. I mentioned, I think, that Lan's feet, too, had once been broken and bound, but she had straightened them. One day early in our time there, while I lay abed resting my sore ankle, Lizzie said to Lan, "Would you mend my feet, Mother, and undo the brokenness?"

"It will be painful, child," Lan replied. "I shall have to break the bones again, and set them straight. It will take time, and much patience."

"How much time?" I asked from the furs. I feared the answer, and it was worse than I expected.

"It shall take twenty days or so, altogether," said Lan. "A day or two to do the breaking and resetting, and twenty for the mending, afore she can walk on them again. That is if all goes well."

"We can't stay that long," I said.

Lizzie sat on a little stool by the fire, and removed her shoes. "Let us begin," she said to Lan.

So they did, there and then. To start with, Lan bathed and massaged Lizzie's feet, softening them with healing oils. Then she began to separate the bent toes from the skin of the soles. All Lizzie's toes, excepting the big ones, had been forced under when her feet were broke, and now they were squashed flat underneath. Separating the skin made Lizzie moan something terrible. Then Lan began to uncurl the toes one by one, making the bones crack, and withdrawing the curved nails from the flesh, where they had grown in. Between workings she applied hot poultices to the convulsed muscles, until the foot was relaxed enough for her to continue. Despite the potion she had taken,

Lizzie sighed and sobbed, rocking in her pain. At last I could abide it no longer.

"Do you have to do this?" I cried, gripping Lan's wrist, stopping her. Lizzie's foot, twisted and twitching in the firelight, dropped into Lan's lap. "'Tis cruel!" I railed. "Leave her be!"

Lan shook me off, took the deformed foot again in her hands, and calmly went on.

"Tell her to stop, Lizzie!" I cried, but she shook her head. She was beyond speech.

"Go outside, boy," said Lan. "You're annoying me, and distressing Jing-wei."

"*I'm* distressing her?" I shouted. "You're the torturer!"

"This is Jing-wei's choice," said Lan. "She wants the brokenness mended. So keep out of it, unless you wish to help."

I did go outside, unable to abide Lizzie's pain.

After, Lan came out and did some work in her garden. I found Lizzie lying on the bed, still groaning. I knelt nearby. "You don't have to suffer this, Lizzie," I said, hoping to stir some sense in her. "Don't let Lan do any more. You've managed all your life with your feet bound. I'll help you go where you want to go."

"For the rest of my life, will you carry me?" she asked.

I thought on that awhile, then mumbled, vexed, "I'm only trying to help you, Lizzie. Only trying to save you from unnecessary pain."

She stopped groaning and glared at me, her chin jutting out stubborn-like. "It's not necessary for me to be able to walk?" she asked. "Is that your sentence on me, Jude of Doran? What of my wishes for myself?"

"'Tis not a sentence!" I cried. "God's bones, you can be contrary, if you set your stupid mind to it! I'm only trotting out my opinion. I have a right to do that, surely, since I'm the one who saved you. If it wasn't for me, you'd still be a freak in a fair!"

"That makes you my new keeper, does it?" she said. "It gives you the right to tell me what to do, how to spend my days, my life?"

I was about to stand up and go, when she said, very quiet and gentle: "I have to do this, Jude. I want to be as other maids."

"You are as other maids," I said, my anger melting. "Better than most."

She smiled then, not as Addy did with mischief and humour, but in a way that was warm and fond, making my heart pound like a drum and my face go red. And that was the last we spoke of the matter.

The next time Lan began to work on her feet, I stayed to help, giving Lizzie her medicines for pain while her foot soaked in potions to soften the skin. Lan had straightened the toes of Lizzie's right foot; this time she would work on the left. Sitting in front of Lizzie again, she laid a towel across her lap, then took Lizzie's crippled foot firmly in her hands. Lizzie breathed in deep, and a determined look came across her, like that of a soldier about to do battle. "Go on with it, Mother," she said.

An hour passed. I don't know how Lizzie endured it. She sat there on that tiny stool, gripping the edges till her hands were white, rocking back and forth and biting her lip till it bled. She did not seem to be aware of me or Lan; I suspect she was locked in her pain, struggling with it in some terrible battleground deep within. Lan told me to get a strip of leather from her chest of healing things, and I did, rolling it into a soft thing for Lizzie to bite upon. Then I stood helpless, while Lan worked and Lizzie moaned. Once Lizzie nearly fainted, and I got another stool and set it behind her and sat close with my front to her back, my arms about her, holding her. She clutched my hands and held them so tight I near cried out myself, but it seemed to give her some relief. And that was the way we always sat after that, when her feet were being mended.

I learned a lot of things, in those long hours I held her in her sufferings. I saw that Lizzie was not a helpless maid I had rescued from a cage. I saw that she was a woman, strong and steadfast, breaking out of a far greater prison than the one I had saved her from. I was not her rescuer; she was saving herself, breaking out of the bondage of restraint and limitation, winning her liberty with awful agony.

They were like journeys, those breaking, healing times, and afterwards we would stay sitting close, Lizzie and I, and she would lean back against me and beg me to talk to her, to say anything to keep her mind occupied. So I told her of my childhood, of the swine I had looked after, my games with Addy and Lucy and the twins, my bumbling efforts with Prue, and my wrangles with her father the miller. Sometimes we laughed, and sometimes we cried. Old Lan never interrupted those talks, but oft went outside leaving us alone in our sharing. In those times I spilled my soul, and never has another human being heard the story of my life and heart as Lizzie heard it then.

Four days it was, before her misshapen feet were new-formed. They looked normal enough by the time Lan finished, though they were bandaged firm to hold the bones in their new places. The evenings I spent making special shoes for Lizzie out of firm leather, that later would be drawn on close about her feet, supporting them all around. Lizzie longed to walk, but Lan forbade it, saying she must rest the bones for twenty days or more, for them to knit together properly.

Those days of waiting were hard for me. My own foot was well mended, and I wanted to be gone, to find a new life for myself, a purpose. Though I saw no evil in Lan, I still feared her company and the knowing way of her. I always felt she read my thoughts, and through all the hours in her home there ran the dread that she had supernatural powers. I think Lizzie laughed secretly at me, knowing my fears, but I could not help them. Even the folk from the village, coming for healing of their toothaches and their hurts, were wary of Lan. They would not come inside her door, but took their medicines from the step, and paid for them with chickens and bags of grain passed cautious-like over the dim threshold. And another thing troubled me: whenever I spoke of leaving, even when the twenty days were almost ended, Lan said Lizzie was not ready yet to walk, and must tarry longer to rest. Also, she thought up tasks she wanted done about her house, like building a wall around her garden to keep out the foxes, mending her stone oven outside, and chopping down a rotten tree behind her house afore it fell in a storm. I did not mind the work, or waiting for Lizzie's healing, but I began to feel again that I was trapped, my stay spun out by Old Lan for reasons I did not know.

Seeking peace, I went to mass one Sabbath at the church in the village, hoping to talk to the priest afterwards; but no one spoke to me, because I stayed at Lan's. Yet I saw folk who had been glad enough of Lan's healing in recent days, so I called them all hypocrites, and went back to Lan's without talking to their priest.

That evening the second thing happened, that made our time at Lan's a turning point. The evening started ordinarily enough: Lizzie and I were sitting near the hearth playing a Chinese game with little pegs of wood poked into holes on a wooden board. Old Lan had a rushlight burning on the wall, and sat beneath it, for she was altering the brown dress I had given Lizzie, to make it fit. It was stifling in the house, and I had a headache and was not in a good humour. Lizzie had just won the third game in a row, and I swept the bits of wood into a pile, ending the competition. Then I noticed that Lan's sewing box, in which she kept her bone needles, hooks and threads, and scraps of fabric, had a dragon painted on the lid.

"Why a dragon?" I asked, getting up and turning the box to the light, so I could see it better. The box was ancient, different from any I had seen, and I supposed it was from China.

"Why not a dragon?" said Lan. "Move, lad; you're in my light."

I stayed where I was, my shadow across her. "Because dragons are evil," said I. "Also, since it was a dragon that wounded your Ambrose, surely you must hate the beasts. I wonder that you have one for decoration."

" 'Twas a dragon that sent Ambrose to me," said Lan, poking me with her scissors, making me shift quick enough. "Besides, dragons are like people, some good, some bad."

"That's heresy," I said. "The Church teaches very plain what is good and what is evil."

"In China," said Lizzie, "dragons are gods, guardians of the sky and keepers of the storms."

"Then the people in China are mistook," said I.

"Are they, now?" remarked Lan, beginning to sew another patch upon a hole. "Are they all mistook, or only a hundred dynasties, and all their wise ones, and all their holy teachers, and even the great Khan himself?"

"A whole nation may be wrong," I said. "Think of the Scots, coming here to murder and plunder and steal our land. And it were the Welsh afore them, causing strife, and afore them the Danes, and the French are always—"

"And you English are golden-hearted and faultless?" said Lan. "You were here from the beginning, were you—never plundered and stole this land yourselves, from someone else?" I said nothing, for my grandfather had never talked about that.

"Your English ways are not the only ways," said Lan, "nor are you all so cunning as you think. You can't even read or write, most of you, and only men of the Church have knowledge; but in my country people are studying at great universities, making music on wondrous instruments, and doing marvellous paintings on silk. While your English soldiers are busy poking enemies with spears and swords, my people are blowing their foes to smithereens with exploding fire. You tell the time by the position of the sun, but in one of our great cities we have a machine, driven by water, that marks time, telling every hour and the moments in between. You flatten animal hides to write upon, but we make fine stuff called paper. And while your monks are still sharpening feathers to copy books slow, one at a time, my people are carving books upon blocks of wood, and printing many copies, quickly and with ease. So don't you tell me my nation is wrong, my people mistook. We have more knowledge, more accomplishments, than you can dream about."

I'm sorry about the feather bit, Brother Benedict; I see it disturbs you. Myself, I think your work is very advanced, and excellent, but I have to tell this tale the way it happened. If you're interested in the Chinese way of bookmaking, you could talk later to Jing-wei, for she knows more about it than I do. Perchance the Abbot will be interested, too.

I wish I had pressed Lan to talk more on such matters, for as it turned out she was wondrous wise; but at the time I was ill-content and full of gloom. Truth to tell, seeing Lan hooking the tiny needle through the fabric, and drawing through the thread, put me in mind of my mother mending clothes for me and the four plagues, and I was hurting in my heart as well as in my head. Also, the picture of the beast on Lan's box awoke in me some dreadful imaginings, and I could not shake them off. Wishing for peace, I pulled off my boots, ready to go to bed. The goat was eating the straw, and as I chased it off, Lan said, "'Tis not as fearsome as you think, Jude."

"Nay, but it eats a fearsome lot," I said.

Lan cackled. "I meant the dragon!" she said. "That's not so fearsome as you imagine."

"I don't imagine it," I lied. And I crawled into the bed and lay watching the smoke swirl about the thatch, thinking on the beast and what it might look like. 'Twould not be like the gorgeous coiled creature on Lan's box, of that I was sure.

"The dragons here, they're not as large as people think they are, nor as cunning," said Lan.

"Have you seen one?" I asked.

"Nay. But Ambrose told me much about them."

I sat up, the better to hear her talk. She was still bent over her sewing, her sparse white hair like a halo in the firelight, her nut-brown skull outlined dark within.

"Ambrose always said that fear was faith in one's enemy," she continued. "He said if one understood that enemy, studied his weaknesses and strengths, where he slept and ate, what his face was like, his weapons, his defence—then the fear vanished. He said knowledge was the greatest weapon of all. And when it came to the fight, he said all that was needed was the right weapon, the right moment, and the steel-strong will to win."

"Little good his knowledge did him," I muttered, "since he was burned half to death."

"But he survived, and passed that knowledge on to me," said Lan. "Nothing in the world is ever wasted, Jude."

I almost laughed. Passed the knowledge on to *her*? God's precious heart! Did she have some mad notion about hunting the dragon herself?

"I know all about dragons and how they may be defeated," Lan said. "I know why the knights failed, most of them. I know our best defence against this present beast, and what is the perfect weapon."

A chill came over me, like a fear. I glanced at Lizzie. She was watching me. There was a curious look on her face, as if she had heard all this before, and now wanted to know my response to the matter. I returned my gaze to Lan. She no longer sewed, but looked across the room at me, her eyes burning in the gloom.

"Jude of Doran, it was fate brought you here to me," she said.

"And fate brought Jing-wei with you. For the weapon I have is something Jing-wei understands well, though you have never heard of it. And the will to win—well, who better to crave the dragon dead than yourself, since it destroyed everything you loved?"

I said nothing, but a coldness clamped across my heart, and I was sure the devil was lurking in that place.

Lan went on: "The dragon must be stopped, Jude. It will go on destroying, until all that is left is a land scorched bare, cities and villages laid waste, and corpses all consumed by flame. And if any folk survive, with burned crops and razed homes and unspeakable wounds—then they will be in such torment that they will beg the Almighty to send the plague, for even that will be a blessed relief.

"I know this, Jude, as sure as I know the sun will rise tomorrow morn. Dragons, once they have tasted human flesh, become twisted in their minds, and must be destroyed. No one else will carry out that task; the king is busy with his battles, and even if some noble knight took it upon himself to slay the beast, he would have no knowledge and would end up worse than my Ambrose did, cooked alive in his armour, and with the dragon still rampant. But we—we have the means to put an end to this calamity, to spare a land from ruin and save a multitude of souls. I tell you true, Jude, 'tis not by chance you stay beneath my roof."

My heart thundered in my breast, and my mouth went dry. Of a sudden I knew what the old hag was hatching; knew, too, that Lizzie was already persuaded, spellbound, and that the mad plot wanted only my consent. I shook my head. I longed to escape, to flee for my life—but I was drowning in the madness of

Lan's eyes, and her words wove about me, bewitching and binding, though I strove with all my soul to shut them out.

"You fear your enemy," she said, "because in the wildness of your imaginings it is huge, hellish, beyond defeat, and 'tis folly to even think of hunting it. But if you saw it true, as it is, in the flesh, you would see that it is but a beast, no wiser than a warhorse, no larger than an ox, no more wicked than a starved dog that hunts for food. I tell you, lad, it would do you good to face the dragon. It would knock that unseemly terror out of you, and give you the strength to take up your true destiny. This task is yours, Jude: for this you alone survived, out of all your village. You'll not rest until you have avenged your family. If you refuse this task, the regret and grief will gnaw at your heart, all your life. I know; I saw the poison that ate at Ambrose, when he failed to do his duty."

At last I tore my gaze from hers, and seized back my wits. "I am not Ambrose, and I have no knightly duty," I said. "And 'tis no unseemly terror, to be afraid of a thing that overnight destroys a village and all its people with it. As for my destiny— that's for God to know, not for you to plot. I'll have no more to do with you, or with this heathen talk. You may have Lizzie under your evil enchantment, but you don't have me."

"There is no enchantment," Lan said, "only a dragon that must needs be slain, and two people who have the means to do it—though one is brave and willing, while the other is a coward."

"I'm no coward!" I shouted, and Lan laughed. Her mockery woke a wild defiance in me, scattering my wits again. "Since you know everything, witch," I said, "and since you think I should face my foe, why don't you call it here, so I can make its acquaintance?"

Lan cackled so much that she rocked back and forth, tears pouring down her cheeks. "You're braver than I thought, lad!" she chortled. "Braver than I thought!"

But brave I was not, only a brazen fool a-tangling with a witch. And well may you splatter your ink, Brother Benedict, and cross yourself right heartily, for the next day something happened that made me know the fullness of her power, the terrible entangling way of her. For the next day—

By corpus bones! There go the bells, for prayer! Quick—be off! Yesterday the Abbot scolded me for making you late sometimes. I'll tidy up here, and blow the candles out. Godspeed!

ELEVEN

HAIL, BROTHER! That was a happy surprise, to be called upon to help harvest the remaining fruit and beans, afore the rains come and settle in for good. 'Twas an ill-planned break, as our story goes, but at least it allowed you more time to spend with Father Matthew, while he struggles between this world and the next. And it gave me time working in the orchard with Jing-wei. She came only in the mornings, for she cannot stand all day. Usually she's busy in the infirmary, so I don't see her excepting in our guest house in the evenings, and that's always overcrowded with pilgrims and noisy children, and there's little peace to talk. I miss her company. And there's no need for you to raise your eyebrows like that, Brother; there's nought between us but friendship. What, you're writing already? Such eagerness! Or mayhap 'tis only obedience to the Abbot's instructions. But I'd best get on with the tale.

That was a bad night at Lan's, after her devilish talk of a dragon hunt. I was unable to sleep for heat and nagging fears, and felt trapped in a trouble too big for me. Worse, Lizzie was entangled in it, too, but she didn't seem to mind. I could hear her calm breathing on the other side of Lan, while I tossed and turned. Even when I did sleep, nightmares tormented me. I was sorely tempted to get up and run away, but terrors of night, and a deep unwillingness to abandon Lizzie, kept me in that bed next to the witch.

In the morning Lan and Lizzie carried on as if there was nought amiss. For the first time Lizzie was allowed to walk a little way, which she did, with Lan on one side and me on the other. Though the walking pained her, she wore a look of joy. She and Lan chatted together, sometimes in their own language. No one spoke of last night's talk, and I felt confused, shut out, as if they shared a secret I knew not. I thought mayhap it was sorcery that bound them, and excluded me. And I confess there was another thing that made me feel alone: the fear that Old Lan might be right, and it was indeed my destiny, and my bounden duty, to slay the dragon and avenge my family. If so, it was a duty I could not face, and in my misery I cursed Lan for pointing it out to me, and myself for being the worthless coward she said I was.

While Lizzie rested I went for a walk past the village fields. The folk were out harvesting their wheat. They sang as they worked, their scythes flashing in harmony in the bright sun, and the peacefulness of the scene eased last night's terrors, though it made me yearn again for Doran, and working beside Prue on our harvest days. And the flashing blades awoke another thing in me: a memory of Tybalt's sword. Then it came to mind what Richard had said about a soothsayer, and a prophecy: that a dragon would come, and be slain by Tybalt's sword.

Oh, Brother Benedict—I cannot tell my relief at that remembering! Joy flooded over me, as if I were a man let out of prison, released from the sentence of death. I almost cheered beside the harvesters in their fields. Old Lan was wrong! It was not my destiny nor my duty to go off hunting for the dragon! She was wrong, her mad ideas all amiss—and I had proof! Almost laughing, I ran back to her house.

She and Lizzie were picking herbs in the garden. I called to Lan, eager to tell her of the prophecy; but the way she stood there among the herbs, her wizened face like a walnut in the bright sun, her almond-shaped eyes shrewd and secretive, made me hesitate.

"Well, boy?" she said. "What's stirred up your pot?"

"A sword," I said. "Tybalt's sword. I remember something I was told about it."

Lan knew of Tybalt, for Lizzie had spoken of her life before we came to Lan's. I was aware of Lizzie, sitting on the little stool she used when in the house, half lost in the bushes of lavender and comfrey. She was very still, listening to what I said.

"Richard told me a prophecy he heard from a soothsayer," I went on, wishing Lan would not look at me as if I were a toad to be tossed into a brew. "The soothsayer said that Tybalt's sword, which his forebears used to slay the last dragons, would slay a dragon again. It would slay the very last of them all."

"And this unknown soothsayer was right, think you?" said Lan.

"Aye," I mumbled, looking away. "It makes sense, what she said."

"And what I say is foolishness?" asked Lan.

I looked at the ground, my tongue stuck to the roof of my mouth.

"I'd take great care if I were you, boy," said Lan, wrathful and quiet. "I cut out the tongues of doubters like you, and fry them on hot stones, and eat them for my supper. Very nice with strips of toad and tarragon sauce."

I heard a muffled sound across the garden, and caught Lizzie laughing, her hand across her mouth, her eyes dancing at me.

Then Lan cackled and bent over her herbs again. "Give us a hand, boy!" she chortled. "Only have a care; I'm very particular about my herbs."

The mirth in the homely garden, the scent of herbs, the ordinary occupation, all worked to ease the fear in me, and made me doubt the seriousness of my situation. Slowly, as I helped Lizzie and Lan in the peaceful garden, it dawned on me that last night's wild talk had been in jest. I even thought that mayhap they both had hatched the plot—pretended to plan a dragon hunt—just to raise my hackles and have fun with me. Fool that I was, for being taken in! I'd lost a night's sleep on account of their trickery! I almost laughed, there in the garden, half admiring their cleverness and the crafty way they'd duped me like a fool.

Well might you laugh, too, Brother Benedict, at their clever trickery—except that I only *thought* right then that it all had been in jest. Hoped it was, more like! Anyway, it was what I believed at the time, and because of my belief I decided it was time to drop that game, and make some proper plans. It occurred to me that since I had lost all in Doran, I had let the world's winds blow me where they willed. It was time to plan my own direction, and think in good earnest on the matter of my life and what I ought to do. I had to think on Lizzie, too, and what might be the best for her, since she seemed disinclined to think on it herself. And so I considered my next moves, while I helped Lizzie pick the herbs.

She explained which plants to pick, and I shared her basket to put them in. It was pleasant work and easy, though several times Lan scolded me for taking too much of a plant, or failing to discard dead leaves. "You don't listen, Jude!" she railed once, hitting me over the head with her shoe.

When she turned away and bent over her bushes again, I raised my right hand and jerked two fingers towards her back. "I've still got my bow fingers, old witch!" I whispered.

"Bow fingers?" said Lizzie, puzzled.

"Aye," I replied, low so Lan would not hear. "My bow fingers. 'Tis a sign of defiance and scorn. I saw soldiers do it, in the taverns. If a man is taken prisoner in battle, his enemies cut off his bow fingers and let him go. Without these two fingers, he can't shoot a bow, and is no threat. Once I saw a lad mock an old war veteran, saying how his days of glory were past, and now he couldn't even chew his food. The old warrior made this sign, saying, 'I've still got my bow fingers, so beware!' I liked the gesture. It's expressive, don't you think? And bold."

"So it is," she said, with a small smile, "except that you told me once that you couldn't shoot a bow to save yourself. So your bow fingers are hardly a threat, Jude."

"Cunning wench," I muttered.

She giggled, and we went on with our task. And all the time

I worked out my plans for the leaving of Lan's house. It was a prudent plan, I thought, fair and fitting for Lizzie as well as for myself, though I confess it caused some sorrow in me, too, for it meant that Lizzie and I must soon part, and I had got accustomed to her company.

Later that day, when Lizzie and I were alone in the garden, tending the little stone oven where Lan baked her bread, I said: "I've been thinking a lot today, Lizzie, about my life and where I'm going with it. I don't wish to tarry any longer at Lan's. Truth to tell, I don't much like the old crone. I never know whether she's in earnest or in jest, and I suspect she torments me just to amuse herself. I feel uneasy here. But you like Lan well enough, and she loves you like a daughter, that's plain as her two teeth. She's of your own people, and you could help each other. Why don't you ask her if you can stay—not just while your feet mend, but after, too?"

Lizzie was silent, poking more sticks into the oven's fire. She did not look at me, but knelt with the smoke swirling about her head, her red-and-green dress gem-bright in the late afternoon sun. She wore that closed, unfathomable look, and I had the feeling I had offended her.

"I'm not abandoning you, Lizzie," I said. "I'll not forget you. I'll visit you as often as I can, I promise. But I have my own life to think about. Well, what say you? Will you stay here with Lan?"

She gave me a strange look, frowning and vexed. "You think that last night's talk was all in jest?" she asked.

"Aye. So it was. That's why I've been thinking on a proper plan, and what we can do with our lives. 'Tis time we talked common sense, Lizzie."

Silent, she bent over the oven again, poking in the wood.

"Lan was playing the fool with me," I said. "That's why she made another joke, when I told her of the soothsayer and the prophecy on Richard's sword. Lan made some wisecrack about cooking up my tongue with bits of toad and tarragon sauce. We all laughed, remember? All that talk of hunting the dragon—it was all a jest, Lizzie! A cruel one, and it went on too long, but it was a jest for all that."

Still she said nothing.

Desperate, I continued: "Richard's soothsayer was not a fool. She foretold two things, and one has come to pass. She foretold a plague of fires that would herald the coming of another dragon. And the second prophecy, that remains yet to be carried out, was that Tybalt's sword would slay the beast. So Lan is wrong."

"So may a prophecy be wrong," said Lizzie. "It takes no cunning to foretell fires in the summertime, and anyone with a long memory could guess that a dragon might be the cause. Richard held on to the prophecy because he's always loved the stories of his forebears and how they slew the dragons. He often said he wished that he were one of them, and could slay a fiery beast. The soothsayer only fired his hope, that's all; it was no prophecy, but a playing on a boy's wild dreams."

Suspecting she was right, I shifted to safer ground. "Well, whether the prophecy is true or no, we still have to get on with our lives," I said. "We have to find somewhere for you to live. You didn't like the idea of a nunnery, and you can't work on a farm with me. Last night Lan talked a lot of foolery, but there was one thing she said aright. It may be that the fates did bring us here, but only so that you could walk again, and find a home. Mayhap this is where you should be, Lizzie. Think on it."

Lizzie's mouth folded in a straight line, and her chin stuck out—a sign of stubbornness I would grow to know well. "Not many days past," she said, "you told me you felt akin to me, that I reminded you of your little sister Addy, and it helped you to help me. You said you'd not make me do anything I was against."

"None of that's changed. I thought you'd like to stay. You're happy here." She said nothing, and I blundered on, hoping to stir some sense in her. "I know Lan told you of a town in the south, where there are several Chinese families. It may be that some are people you know, from the ship you came on. If you want to go to them, I'll come back and take you there, when your feet are properly healed. But I'll not tarry here longer. I'm going on the morrow. This time I mean it."

Poker-faced, she stood up, then stumbled. I reached out to steady her, but she pulled away. "Lan was right," she said, cold as frost. "You've a faint heart, Jude of Doran." Then she turned and began limping back to the house.

"And *your* heart is fickle!" I bellowed after her. "You've changed! You were a more pleasant maid when you were in your cage!"

To my astonishment she turned around and raised her bow fingers to me. Then she vanished into the house.

Swearing, I shoved more sticks into the oven, and purposed in my heart to leave Lan's on the morrow, whether Lizzie liked it or no. I tell you, Brother Benedict, women are mighty hard to fathom at times, and you can thank your stars you have no dealings with them. Lizzie still bewilders me sometimes, and vexes me, though she's a lamb compared to Old Lan.

The evening was tranquil, I remember, the air ringing with the songs of crickets and birds. It is uncanny, how one remembers little details. There was a tiny grass-snake by the oven, drawn no doubt by the sweet scent of baking bread. Across the dusty grass-lands that surrounded Lan's house I could see the golden fields, near shorn of all their wheat, and the church tower beyond. Those were the last moments of my peace, such as it was.

Of a sudden, all went quiet. I stopped tending the fire and looked up. High in the violet skies was a great bird. I thought of the eagles my grandfather had spoken of, which he saw on his travels north; and I watched, entranced. Slowly the bird flew down, lower and lower, and I saw, with heart thundering and terror crashing over me, that it was not a bird but a winged lizard, aglow like copper in the sunset fire.

"Holy Jesus, save us!" I prayed, and got up, stumbling backwards to the house, my eyes never leaving the horror in the skies. Before I reached the door I felt Lizzie at my side, and Lan with us.

"Keep silent, don't move," whispered Lan. "'Tis only after my bread. It's already eaten well—you can see its belly swollen and full. With any luck it'll come right down, and you'll get a good eyeful."

Corpus bones! Was she afraid of nothing? I wanted to scream, to howl, to run, but Lan gripped my arm and held me fast.

Down and down the dragon came, drifting slow, now and then beating its wide wings. It circled directly over our heads, and I could see wisps of smoke puffing from its wide nostrils. Its amber wings seemed parchment-thin and smooth, and the light shone through between the dark lines marking sinews and bones. But the rest of the beast glittered with scales, multi-coloured and coppery, sheen of tawny gold shot through with purple and turquoise and orange. Even through all my hate and fear, I thought that it was beautiful.

The dragon flew on, was lost beyond the branches of the trees behind Lan's house. As still as stones, we waited for it to appear again. But it did not. It was still overhead somewhere, hidden by the trees and the steep roof of Lan's house. All around, the earth was uncannily still, quiet as death. Then I noticed a shadow sliding along the ground, from behind us. Larger it grew, and larger, purple-blue on the shining grass. There was no sound; just that dreadful shadow coming ever nearer, increasing, from somewhere behind the house. Then a sound, velvet-soft, like a huge breath being expelled, and wind whistling over wings. At that moment it appeared, directly over our heads, so close I could have tossed a stone at it. Across the garden it flew, over the grass, then turned just before it reached the village fields, and came back, only the height of a man above the earth. Its breath shimmered; before it the grass bent, caught alight, little flames running before the heat. The sunset air was full of tiny fires, insects flying with their wings alight, then drop-ping, scorched, upon the grass. Smoke drifted, stinking of sulphur.

Then the dragon landed, wings spread wide to break the flight. It dropped, touched the grass, and stopped. It was just on the other side of Lan's garden.

My heart hammered as if it were about to leap out of my breast. I could hear Old Lan muttering under her breath, and hoped she prayed, or else was making the strongest spell that ever was made by a witch. I tell you, Brother Benedict, at times like that it doesn't matter much who helps—God or the devil.

The dragon came nearer, its head moving low along the ground, side to side, sniffing. Every time it breathed, it scorched a trail of fire across the earth. Its neck was long, graceful, and glittering like gold. Its wings were folded close against its brilliant body, the wing sections shiny and ribbed like fish fins, the fine bones ending in sharp hooks. The long barbed tail was bent, the bones set crookedly, yet it coiled and uncoiled as slowly and smoothly as a snake. All the dragon's movements were smooth, fluid and fascinating, almost spellbinding in their beauty and their deadliness. Its body and head were the size of those of a large horse; but the length of its neck and tail, and the breadth of its wings when they were outstretched, gave it fearsome size.

My breath hurt in my throat, and I felt dizzy and sick. Sweat trickled down my face and neck, and I could not stop shaking. I dared not take my eyes off the dragon's head. Smoke clung all about, and I could smell the awful stench that had hung over Doran that fateful day. As the creature came nearer I could hear its scales sliding across one another, sounding like silk, softer and more treacherous than a sword being drawn from its scabbard. I saw its scarlet eyes, ringed in scales like a lizard's eyes. Paralysed, I waited. It was looking right at me, surely! It would breathe soon, and Lizzie and Lan and I and the house would be cinders.

But the dragon moved away, its head low to the ground, sniffing, its forked tongue licking the grass, tasting the air and the smoke laden with the scent of bread. Finding the oven, it clawed aside the stones and found the bread. It ate everything—burned wood and dough, even the ashes and some of the smaller stones. I could see its jaws moving, hear the splintering of wood and grinding of teeth. As the dragon ate it breathed out ash and blue fumes, and in the hush the slow expulsion of breath sounded harsh and terrible. The air reeked of dragon-fire.

And then, its meal complete, the beast simply leaped into the evening air, and flew away.

Lan rushed into the house, got a blanket, and began beating out the little fires that were spreading through the grass. I collapsed against the wall of her house and covered my face with my hands, trying to shut out the sight, the memories of Doran, the thoughts that tortured me. And through all the horror and grief there rose an awful hate, powerful beyond words.

When next I opened my eyes, Lizzie was helping Lan with the fires, limping to and fro betwixt Lan and the well, carrying buckets of water. When they had finished, Lan passed close by me on her way back into the house.

"I should have poisoned my bread, Jude!" she cackled. "We could have lived on dragon steaks till Christmastide!"

Something shattered in me, and I shouted, "Witch! You called it here! You called it, with your spells and enchantments and devil-powers! Why didn't you kill it, while you had it? For God's love—you lived with a knight who told you all the tricks! You said you could kill the thing—why didn't you? Why let it fly off to burn another village, and slaughter more people? How could you let it go like that, and then jest? How can you *jest*?" I was babbling, half out of my wits with terror and hate and rage.

Lan drew herself up to her full height. She barely reached my chest. "I didn't slay it, Jude," she said, with deadly calm, "because I was not ready. There is a certain amount of preparation, before my weapon can be used. But I shall make those preparations, if that's your wish. Jing-wei knows the power of what I have to use, and knows how it is best harnessed. She would go, if you would carry her there."

"Go?" I said, stupidly. "Go where?"

"To the coast where the dragon dwells. I'm a little old for such a journey. But you could make it. You and Jing-wei, together. You could kill the beast."

"Aye, for sure!" I said, trying to laugh. "I can just see that—a fiery beast slaughtered by a village oaf who can't shoot a barn at twenty paces, and a crippled maid! And what shall we do after that—go and conquer Scotland?"

"You talk like a fool," she said. "And Jing-wei is no crippled maid. If anyone is crippled here, 'tis you."

Lan went inside, and I stormed off—

Oh, Brother, there go the bells again! Have done, begone, no time to waste! I swear I'll get straight into the tale tomorrow, no idle gossip first!

twelve

S PROMISED, STRAIGHT into the tale!

I was sorely tempted to leave Lan's there and then, for I'd endured about as much as I could take from that old witch; but I could not go without Lizzie. I was mortal scared that Old Lan had indeed enchanted her, and her wits were gone. And if Lan had been serious in her talk about the dragon hunt, then she was mad, or demon-possessed, and mortal dangerous. Nothing would save Lizzie now, excepting I carried her away.

She was standing by the step, just outside the door. Though it was almost dark by then, I could see by the starlight that her face was calm and solemn, and her hands were folded in her sleeves. It was the way she had stood that day I first saw her, on the platform in Tybalt's tent. A thousand summers ago, it seemed.

"Lan's dangerous," I said, very low. "She's put a spell on you, the same way she bewitched the dragon to come down here, and then to leave without causing strife. She's a witch, Lizzie.

Can you not see that? We should go afore we both get entangled in her sorceries, and this folly gets worse. Will you come with me now? I'll carry you. And I'll help you to walk a little way each day, as Lan advised. Your healing will go on. You'll lose nothing by leaving with me now, save witchery."

"I will not go," she said. "Lan is no witch, only a woman wise in science and alchemy, and in things not yet invented in this backward land. There is a weapon we can use, long used in China, which I know about. And the dragon was not called here, any more than it was called to Doran or to the other places it destroyed. It came by chance, drawn by the smell of baking bread. Forget your fear, Jude. We can kill this beast, you and I."

"Tell me you jest," I said.

But she remained grave as a nun.

"By Jesus' blessed tree, you *are* bewitched!" I cried. "Either that, or else you're a lunatic, mad as Lan! I'll not be trapped here with you, bewitched into a plot that can only lead to death! I'm off."

"If you go, you'll never have peace," she said. "Lan was right about that. You will forever blame yourself that you knew how to slay the thing that destroyed your family, yet did nothing."

"Why should you care?" I asked, harsh because she spoke the truth.

She was silent for so long that I tried to see her face, to read her feelings there; but she looked away, biting her lip, and I supposed she was angry with me.

"This is farewell, then," I said. "I'll come and see you sometime, if you wish."

"Of course I wish it, Jude," she said, very quiet. "Where will you go?"

"Anywhere," I said. "Anywhere save here. I'll find work, become a swineherd again, mayhap."

In the dark doorway behind Lizzie, Old Lan appeared, snorting. "Forget the boy, Jing-wei," she said. "He's a fainthearted fool, crippled by his fear, afraid to face his destiny. Let him go back to his pigs. I'll go with you, and together we shall slay the beast. We'll have Ambrose's brave spirit on our side, and his hard-won wisdom. We'll finish the work that he began. 'Tis a fine enough reason for us to go, daughter."

"I know another fine reason!" I cried, furious. "You'll rid the world of a witch, and that's no small accomplishment! 'Tis a pity you'll take a hapless maid with you, though."

Without a word Lan hobbled back inside. Lizzie went with her, not even stopping to say farewell, or to wish me Godspeed.

Shaking with helpless rage, I walked away, past the burned ground in the garden, towards the shorn fields, the church tower, and the village. The force of my anger was frightening, overwhelming, like a furnace melting all my fear and guilt and grief into white-hot hate. I stopped on the blackened earth where the beast had been, and thought of Doran blackened on that fateful day, and Lizzie's words drove into me like knives.

Swearing, I turned and strode back to the house. They had closed the door, so I flung it open with such force that it crashed against the wall. Lan was hacking at vegetables with an evil-looking knife, and Lizzie was sitting on a stool before the fire, her cheeks streaked with tears.

Stopping on the step, half out of my wits with despair and rage, I said two words that altered all my life. "I'll go," I said.

Lizzie half stood, a smile breaking like the dawn across her face. Then she sat down again, her hands in her lap, upturned. Her gaze was on me still, and the look in her face, the joy, the smile on her, is the kind of look every lad longs for from a maid. I remember wondering, in those strange, fateful moments, if every maid would smile like that on a lad who pledged himself to die for her. Little wonder the knights were so courageous at the tournaments I'd heard about, willing to spill their blood for a lady's love.

Lan put down her knife and came and stared into my face, so close I could smell the stink of her breath. She was not smiling.

"You've an inconstant heart, Jude of Doran," she said. "Your moods are fickle, now up, now down, like buckets in a well. How do I know you won't change your mind? That you won't abandon Jing-wei halfway through the quest?"

"I plight my word," I said. "I'd rather go with her, even if I die, than let her go with you."

"Swear it," she said. "Swear by all you believe in, that you'll be Jing-wei's true and steadfast friend, that you'll go with her to the dragon's lair, and do all that she says, without argument."

"I wouldn't count on that last," I said.

"But I do count on it, Jude," she said, leaning too close for comfort. "The souls of your dead kin count on it, and Jing-wei counts on it, and it is counted much upon by all the folk you're going to save. So will you do as Jing-wei says, the moment she asks, without question or argument?"

God's soul, I could swear her eyes were alight! I wanted to look away, and could not. I was trapped in that fiery bloodred stare of hers, paralysed and helpless, like a fly in a web.

At last I found my tongue. "Aye," I said. "I'll do as she says."

"Swear it," Lan said.

A long time it took, afore the words were out of me. "I swear it, on God's cross and my salvation."

"'Tis done, then!" Lan crowed, triumphant.

And so it was. I pledged my soul, Brother Benedict, to obedience without question. I see you nod, solemn-like, knowing vows like that. At least you made your vows to the Abbot and to God. I made mine to a wizened crone and a crippled maid so full of mystery and secrets that the vowing felt like the signing of the warrant to my own death.

THIRTEEN

REETINGS, BROTHER. You look worn out. Jing-wei told me you sat with Father Matthew all night, and that he clings to this world, still. Are you sure you want to do this work with me today? You do? Very well. But sign if you want to stop, for well I know the weariness that sorrow brings.

I see you've been drawing again, along the top of the page. A dragon, and remarkably well done, too! But if you don't mind my saying so, there needs to be a horn at the end of its nose, between its nostrils. 'Tis about the length of your quill, the horn. You can draw it in later, and then your picture will be wonderfully true to the real creature.

Meanwhile, I'll tell you of the plot that Old Lan made for the slaying of it.

That very night, with the three of us around the fire, she told Lizzie and me of her scheme. Deep-laid it was, shrewd and purposeful, and I had the feeling that she'd heard it long ago from

Ambrose, and held it in her heart, and dwelled on it long nights of late, while the dragon ravaged our land. She was excited, telling of it, zealous and exact, like a king plotting war.

"You have to know your enemy," she said, "so I'll tell you all that Ambrose told me. First, know the dragon's three great strengths: fire, swiftness, and flight. Its fire you already know—you've seen what it can do. What you didn't see tonight was its swiftness. Ambrose said a dragon can turn a circle upon a single foot; you might come up behind it, but afore you blink, it will have spun about and covered you with its fire. And it flies very quiet, for 'tis light, and can drift great distances without a sound. And those are its only strengths.

"So listen well, Jude of Doran, for now you will learn its weaknesses, and by these you will gain the mastery. The dragon has no great brain, and is not cunning, as wolves and wildcats are. Neither does it see well. Its eyes are on either side of its head, and it sees nothing straight in front of it, but has to turn its head to see about itself, and then it sees things distorted, from the side, as it were. It cannot judge distances aright, and uses far-flung fire to catch its prey, as a spider spreads a web. Its hearing is not good, but it knows a man's approach by the tremor of his footsteps in the ground. Its best sense is its smell, and by that it hunts. That is why it flies at day's end, when cooking-fires send up their smoke, signalling where the villages are. This dragon that we saw needs easy prey, such as humans, for it has never learned from a parent how to hunt the wild mountain beasts or the creatures of the sea. It is but young, small yet, and unsure how to kill except by fire. It's not vindictive or evil, else it would have killed us tonight, afore it flew away. 'Tis only after food. And, in spite of all the tales, dragons are not bold. They will fly off sooner than fight, though they are fierce enough when threatened—as are we all. They are sorely misunderstood, and should never have been hunted out of existence. Ambrose himself said that, with deep regret."

"Mayhap this one, too, is only misunderstood, and should not be hunted," I said, hoping to stir some doubt in the old crone. "Mayhap Ambrose would wish us to leave it well alone, for it may grow to hunt a different prey, and leave off killing folk."

Lan cackled. "You don't wriggle out of it that easily, boy," she said. "Your dragon has tasted human flesh and found an easy prey. There'll be no changing of its ways. It has to be destroyed. And the power to do that lies in Jing-wei's knowledge, and in your hands."

"Then you'd better show me," I said. "What is this weapon we have, that cannot fail?"

Lan got up and hobbled over to a corner, the farthest from the fire. Taking the curved bone she used for digging in her garden, she began digging up the earthen floor. Not far beneath the beaten surface was a wooden board, and this she pulled up, with some difficulty. I supposed it had not been moved for many a year. From a hole beneath she pulled a bag, well wrapped in rags. Then she came back to the firelight, but sat a safe distance from the flames. Lizzie leaned forward upon her stool, her face eager and intent. I tried not to look too eager, though I was all atremble. What mystery was here, what powerful witchery?

Carefully Lan untied the twine about the sack's opening, and took out a round bundle wrapped well with thick skins. Several layers there were, some of the skins still with fur, and of animals unknown to me. Last of all was a bundle wrapped in black cloth, strong and close-woven. This she also opened, and before us there lay a pile of dust. Or sand. Or ash, or anything, save weaponry.

"What's this?" I cried. "A jest, to wind me up? By God's belly and blood, you push me too far!"

Lizzie laid her hand upon my arm. "Peace, Jude," she said. "It looks harmless enough, but this dust has more death in it than twenty swords."

I looked at Lan; she was smiling a little, amused. Witch! You're enjoying this, I thought. Leaning over, I took a pinch of the powder, and sniffed it. It smelled like nothing I knew.

"Is it poison?" I asked, brushing the stuff from my fingers, lest I die of a sudden.

"Nay," said Lan. "'Tis something yet unknown in this land. But for hundreds of years it has been known in my land, and Jing-wei knows of it, and full well she knows its strength. There is destruction in every particle. It burns, this powder, Jude. And when it burns, it burns with unspeakable violence, with the sudden strength of a mighty wind. And if there are, placed within this powder, bits of sharp steel or flint, then these are flung out with such force that they tear to pieces everything in their path. Even armour is pierced, and shields, and wood. I have seen enemy soldiers so mangled that there was nothing left but tattered, bloody flesh. And not one man only is destroyed in such a blast, but many. 'Tis like letting loose a thousand hellish blades all at once, in the blinking of an eye. Nothing survives such a blast—not even a dragon."

I moved away from the dust, and Lan chuckled as she

wrapped it away again within its cloths and skins. "'Tis safe enough for now," she said. "It needs fire to set it off. That's why it's wrapped so well. One spark is all it needs. But you are right to move away. This dust belongs to Jing-wei, and will not be touched again by you."

"What happens if it doesn't have the flints and steel in it?" I asked. "Is it all fire and wind?"

"Something like that," said Lizzie. "By itself, with coloured powders mixed in it, and shot high into a night sky, it makes beautiful fire-flowers. They are brighter than the moon, and can be seen for miles around. My father used to make them on the nights of great festivals, and for celebrations. But mixed with sharpened steel, and set alight close to enemies, 'tis deadly. I know how to set it off, Jude. I used to watch my father make the fire-flowers, when I was a child. He took great care, though, for sometimes there were accidents and people were badly burned. Handled with skill, the dust is a weapon that will conquer any foe."

"And what if it kills us, too?" I said. "What protection do we have against it?"

"Distance," said Lan. "I'm hoping that even you won't be fool enough to stand right next to it with a flaming torch, boy. You place the bundle of steel and powder in the entrance to the dragon's lair, and the dragon itself will set it alight with its fiery breath. And then all will be over, in less time than you can blink."

"What if the beast won't go near to it?" I asked. "What if it won't breathe on it?"

"Then Jing-wei knows of another way. Mayhap you will have

to wait until the dragon sleeps, and place the bundle next to it. I'll show Jing-wei how to make a long trail with dry rags, leading to the bundle of powder. The trail of rags can be as long as needed. Then you hide in a place of protection, and set the rags alight. The fire will creep along them to the bundle of powder and steel, and afore the dragon knows what is happening, it will be pierced to its fiery heart as if by a hundred fatal swords. 'Tis all a matter of timing."

"I don't think I want to touch the stuff," I muttered. "It's from the pits of hell."

"It may seem like magic to you now, Jude," said Lan, "but not a hundred years hence, this powder will be on every battleground in England."

She put the bag of death away in its hole, covered it up, then brought back something else from one of her shelves. It was a pot of flints and shards of steel. I had noticed it before, when I was poking about when she was out, and thought she used the flints and shards to torture frogs, or to stick into effigies of enemies, to put doom-spells on them.

"Ambrose collected these," Lan said. "There are more than two hundred shards in here—enough to deal a fatal injury to your dragon, I'll warrant."

"Ambrose collected them?" I asked. "Was he going to use your fire-dust?"

"Aye, he thought of it," she said. "When he was here, there were still a few dragons about, and one—an old wounded beast—made trouble hereabouts. It were more than sixty winters past, now. But he . . . he died afore he had the chance. I kept all these things, in case this need should arise."

"This is all to do with Ambrose, isn't it?" I said, suddenly angry. "'Tis nothing to do with helping me avenge my family, or saving folk from the dragon. This is to try out Ambrose's crack-brained plot! This is all for *his* sake!"

"'Tis not crackbrained!" she spat, standing up over me with the pot of shards still in her hands. I thought she was going to break it over my head. "One day, Jude," she said, "you'll be thankful for all that the fates have done for you."

To my great relief she put away the pot with its deadly contents, but came back with a small jar that smelled of healing oils. This she gave to me, and told Lizzie to sit down. "I'll teach you to massage Jing-wei's feet, to keep them supple and ease the pain in them," she said to me. "You must do it twice a day, then bandage her feet firm again, to keep them mending straight. Sit in front of her. That's right. Now, remove her shoes and bandages."

It was an odd lesson, massaging a maid's feet. Lan showed me which way the muscles lay, and how to work with them and not against them. She told me the places to avoid, where bones had been reset, and showed me how to flex the toes to help ease them in their new positions. Where skin had been broken I learned to oil the scars well, to prevent them from contracting and causing the feet to curl under again. I was right earnest about the task, wanting to do well, but Lizzie laughed at times, mayhap because my unfamiliar hands tickled. I was glad to give her some pleasure, after all she had been through.

After, when the fire burned low and we were sipping bowls of ale and thinking of sleep, Lan said, "Tomorrow we'll talk of your journey, and how you can find out where the dragon dwells."

"I already know where it lives," I said. "I heard a minstrel describe the place. 'Tis on the western coast, in St. Alfric's Cove. Men on a passing ship gave report of it."

"Do you know where this cove is?" asked Lan.

"I've forgot," I replied, allowing myself a brief, wild hope that that might end the matter.

"It is past the city of Twells," said Lizzie. Seeing my surprise, she smiled a little and added, "I was listening to the minstrel, too, that night. There's a little village on the edge of the cliff, over-looking the cove. It keeps a fire burning every night, to warn ships away, since so many were wrecked there in times past."

"It should not be too difficult to find, once you have directions to Twells," said Lan. "It seems, then, that you have all the knowledge you need."

I was sorely tempted to point out that it was courage I needed, not knowledge, but I closed my mouth. Looking at me sharp, Lan said, "We all have dragons to conquer, one way or another, Jude. Have no fear; you will be well prepared. All this was written in your stars."

And talking of what is written, Brother Benedict, I think you've done enough for this day.

I'll bring Jing-wei after supper, and she can tell you more about her country, if you wish, and about their ways of making books. Mayhap the Abbot would like to hear her, too; he's zeal-ous about his dream that everyone will read, and determined to increase by a hundredfold the books in your library here. The scriptorium is crowded, as he's training twenty more brothers to copy manuscripts. There's parchment aplenty, he says, and ink, but the quills are running short. The geese in your monastery farmyard are overplucked, and are becoming devilish difficult to catch, and he's asking all the guests who come to spread the word that he will take a goose in payment for hospitality here, instead of money. He's so full of zeal, I didn't like to point out that the farmyard may soon be overburdened with too many geese. I suppose he'll discover that himself, when they start cluttering up the cloisters and honking through the hallelujahs.

I'd wipe that smile off your face if I were you, Brother— you've got sixty books to copy out when this one of ours is done!

FOURTEEN

 UNDERSTAND WHY you're late, Brother; please don't apologise. Jing-wei told me that Father Matthew died last night. I'm sorry; I know you loved him well. I heard that his funeral is tomorrow. Do you think the Abbot would mind if Jing-wei and I joined in the ceremonies, seeing as she looked after him in the infirmary? We seem to share so much of your lives here, we would regret missing this important occasion.

And now, on with my own important occasion, since you're willing to continue writing today—though even a dragon hunt seems insignificant compared with a soul entering heaven.

The next day Lizzie and I prepared to leave Old Lan's. Though I had prayed all night for storms and earthquakes and floods and even an onslaught from the Scots, the day was like every other day this summer past—windless and still, and blazing hot.

Lan took great care packing our provisions, for we were to

take food for the journey, as well as the bag of fire-dust and the shards of steel and flint, wrapped now in heavy cloth, and the jar of oil for massaging Lizzie's feet. I say *we* were to take them, though in truth it was I who was to carry everything, including Lizzie. I managed to hold my peace, until I saw Lizzie roll her red silken dress into a bundle, with her tiny shoes she no longer needed, and poke them into the bag with the cloaks and blankets.

"I'm not taking those as well," I said. "You don't need your silk dress, and you'll never wear those little shoes again."

"I'm not leaving them behind," she said. "They are all I have of my family."

"But we can come back here after, if we survive. You can get them then."

"We're travelling south," she said, "to the village Lan has told me of. 'Tis pointless coming back again all this way."

"The maid speaks true," said Lan, coming over with her wooden sewing box. Opening it, she selected several balls of fine cord, some large needles, and her evil-looking scissors. These she wrapped in several strips of cloth, and poked into the bag with the silk dress.

"*Embroidery* gear?" I cried, outraged. "You must be daft if you think I'm taking that!" I reached into the bag and grabbed them out.

Lan gripped my wrist, so hard her nails cut my skin. "You will carry whatever we say you will carry," she hissed, breathing garlic and leek. "Those embroidery threads may be vital. You swore obedience, remember."

She released me, and I rubbed my wrist and said nothing,

though in my heart I ranted and raved enough. I managed to hold my peace yet again when Lan packed another jar of oil and a container of ointment, explaining that they were to put on burns, should we receive them. When all was packed there were two bags, each as heavy as a large side of pickled pork. I thought on the journey here from Tybalt's fair, and how weary and foot-sore I had got carrying Lizzie all that way, though she was light.

"I'll be worn out afore I get there," I said gloomily, "carrying these and Lizzie besides."

"It doesn't matter if you are worn out," said Lan. "Once there, your usefulness is past. Jing-wei can do everything."

"Oh, that thrills me to the veins, that does!" I cried. "So I'm to be her donkey, nothing more!"

"You can be more, if you've the nerve for it," said Lan, tying twine tight about the necks of the two bags. "But you're ham-pered by a mighty contrary disposition, Jude of Doran."

"I think my disposition is warranted," I said, "since Lizzie and I are off to make dragon fodder of ourselves."

Lizzie laughed, covering her mirth with her hand. Despair broke over me, and I stormed outside. While there, doing battle with my doubts, I spied a donkey coming along the road towards Lan's house. The beast was sorely burdened with a woman almost larger than itself. Two men walked with them, one on either side, supporting the woman. As they left the road and turned towards Lan's house, I saw that the woman looked near death, she was so white, and her leg, sticking out from beneath her blood-stained skirt, was wrapped in rags soaked scarlet.

Seeing me, the older man called, "Get Lan for me, lad! 'Tis my wife, cut awful bad with a scythe. Make haste!"

I ran back to the house, but Lan had heard and was already taking boxes of rags and jars of potions from her shelves. Seeing me, she said, "Don't stand there gawking, boy! Help the men bring her in!"

I went outside and helped the men lift the woman from the donkey's back. It was no easy task, for she was near fainting, and was a cumbersome soul to move. She fell off, in the end, and it took the three of us to drag her across Lan's threshold and over near the fire. The older man unwound the bindings from her shin, and I saw a cut deep, and gone bad with blackness and pus. A foul smell wafted up from it.

"Throw the bindings in the fire," said Lan. The man did as he was bid, then stepped back. Unwilling-like, he tarried in the doorway with the other man, a younger version of himself.

"When did this happen?" asked Lan, kneeling beside the woman.

The husband hung his head. "About two days past," he muttered.

"Fool!" cried Lan. "Why did you not bring her straight-away?"

"Well, to be true . . . It were the morning after the dragon came. We saw it land hereabouts, and thought . . . Well, Good Mother, I was afeared that—that—"

"You were afeared I'd called the thing down here to slobber in my bucket, so I could make spells with dragon spit!" raged Lan. "Is that it, man?"

He stood red-faced and sheepish, looking at the ground. But his son, a bright-looking lad, said eagerly, "Aye, that was it, Mother! We were sure it were your familiar! We only brought

Mama 'cos she's sickened worse, and like to die, and no one else can help."

"We'll pay you well," said the older man. "We have swine, and chickens, and—"

"The donkey," I said, in a moment of inspired cunning. "Lan will take your donkey."

"Not the donkey," said the man. "Please, not the donkey."

Lan looked at me, winked, then said to the man, "'Tis the donkey, or I'll not help your wife. And if I don't help her, she'll die."

"Anything but my donkey," the man said. "I've had him five summers, and he's as a son to me. I couldn't—"

"You can't keep both," said Lan. "Your donkey or your wife? Which do you want?"

The man groaned, wringing his huge hands in despair, and was a long time undecided.

Then of a sudden his wife sat up. I don't know where she got the strength, for she was like a corpse; but she looked daggers at him and said, with awful ire, "One more moment's doubt, and I'll flay you alive, Jonah Smollet." Then she fell back, fainted clean away, and the ground shook at her falling.

Jonah Smollet sighed deep. "You'd best have the donkey," he said.

And that was how Lizzie and I came to have a donkey for our journey. 'Twas a well-timed gift, to be sure, and I was grateful for it, though the owner went away sorely disgruntled. While Lan set about cleaning up the woman's cut, Lizzie and I finished packing our things. We put a thick folded blanket on the donkey's back, tied the sacks of supplies together with ropes, and slung them across. When all was ready, Old Lan came out to see us off. She and Lizzie embraced heartily, and Lizzie vowed to come back sometime and visit her.

"Nay—you'll be busy with other things, when you've done with the dragon," said Lan. "I'll know how you be, and where you be. You've great joy ahead, dear one."

They embraced again, and I think the old crone would have hugged me, too, had I not stepped back right quick.

Lan wished me Godspeed, and her last words to me I never forgot, for their strangeness: "Remember, Jude, the worst dragons are the ones in your mind."

Then I lifted Lizzie onto the donkey's back and picked up the rope that was about its neck, and we set off. Lizzie looked back many times, and waved farewell. I never looked back at all. I set my face to the way ahead, and felt like a man heading off on a journey to his own hanging.

Don't look so gloomy, Brother; we did not go to our deaths, obviously, else I would not be sitting here upon this stool, telling you the tale. And our journey was pleasant enough, if you forgot the minor detail of the dragon at the end of it. Our road wound between small woods and green hills marching westward, dotted with the spires of distant villages; and the coast was far off yet. Besides, I had the company of a comely maid, and a cheerful one.

Talking of company, I've just remembered something else. New visitors arrived here at the monastery today. I've not seen them myself, but they're being housed in the west wing of the guest house, where the nobles stay, so they must be grand. They're Easterlings, I've heard; merchants from the Indies, Persia, and China. They're travelling together for safety, and between

them they have twenty horses and fifty hounds, and forty servants or more. The Abbot won't like housing the hounds, I'll
warrant, with all his precious geese safely ensconced in the barn.
He has enough to worry about, with Father Matthew's funeral
to be organised. I'll see you there, tomorrow? Meanwhile, I'll say
a prayer for Father Matthew's soul, and one for all of you who
loved him.

FIFTEEN

WELL, FATHER MATTHEW IS IN heaven now, sent on his way with so much love and singing and ceremony, 'twas enough to break a heart.

Today's ceremonies meant more to me than you know, Benedict. For during them I realised that I had never said farewell to Mama and Father, to my grandfather, or to little Addy, Lucy, and the twins. I'd carried a terrible pain within me, ever since that last day in Doran, and have never laid it down—until today.

Today I laid it down, out in the garden at Father Matthew's grave. In my heart I buried them there with him. Only they weren't buried; I think their souls were flying upwards in the autumn wind, free at last. As I am free.

I cannot talk anymore today; my heart is too full. We'll continue with this story on the morrow. 'Tis St. Jude's day tomorrow—the day of my patron saint. Mayhap he knows my story, too, and has given me the blessing of his peace.

Brother, what a lot has happened since last we met! As it was St. Jude's day yesterday, the Abbot asked Jing-wei and me to have supper at his table. So we did; but we weren't the only guests. He asked the Easterlings as well, so Jing-wei met the Chinese merchants. Two brothers they are, one old as you, perhaps, one not many summers older than I. The younger one is called Chen. He deals in purple silk, sandalwood, nutmegs and other rare spices, as well as spikenard and ebony. He wears silk gowns richly embroidered, and has long hair like Jing-wei's, pulled back in a tight glossy plait. He speaks English well enough, though his accents are strange, for he's not been travelling in this country more than a year, and he has a quaint way of saying things at times. He told us that he comes from Hangchow, the same city that Lizzie lived in, when—

No need to sigh like that, Benedict! I'll get on with my story. I just thought you might be interested, for Chen told us some amazing tales. My own journey to the coast is mild, compared with Chen's travels—though he's never fought a dragon, that I know, nor even seen one. Jing-wei told him, briefly, what we'd done, and he was speechless with amazement—and he wasn't often speechless. All right, all right—I'll get on with it.

So, we travelled with our donkey through the countryside, westward to the coast. The journey was mainly uneventful. We ate frugally twice a day, to make our supplies last, and filled our water skins from streams. We passed through several villages, but did not talk to the people there, save to ask directions to Twells, for Lizzie had commanded me not to tell a soul of our quest. Lan had said the same thing, and I saw the sense of it. I had no wish to be taken for mad and thrown in chains—or, worse, to have devils beaten out of me. At night we slept on our blankets under hedgerows or beneath trees, with the donkey between us. Of a night Lizzie told wondrous tales: madcap things that happened when she lived with the Gypsies, or curious legends her mother had passed on to her, from China, or stories she made up herself when she was caged, to make the captivity bearable. I loved her wit, her way of lifting my heart and making me laugh. And yet sometimes I'd say or do a thing she disagreed with, and then she'd vent her ire on me, right forcefully.

One evening while we were sitting on the grass facing one another, and I was massaging Lizzie's feet the way Lan taught me to, we saw the dragon flying overhead, away from the coast. Though it was high up we could see its belly glow with inner fire against the stars. Me it struck with mortal fear, but Lizzie watched it in wonder.

"'Tis beautiful," she sighed. "When I was a child I loved dragons. Our Chinese dragons are different from your English ones. Yours are dangerous beasts, creatures to be feared. Ours are gods to us, symbols of good luck and power."

"You'll find it hard to kill one, then," I said, only half in jest. "Mayhap we should forget this mad quest, spare ourselves a great deal of trouble, and save our skins besides."

"You swore you'd not abandon this quest, Jude!" she said. "You swore it! If you go back on your word—"

"God's nails and blood! I only spoke in jest," I muttered.

"Liar," she said, and shoved me in the chest with her oiled foot, making me tumble backwards. When I recovered, she was laughing at me. She was a strange mixture, was Lizzie, of sweetness and defiance, child-like joy and self-control so unbending it was fearsome.

I forget how many days we journeyed. Nine or ten altogether, perhaps. The further west we got, the barer the roads and fields became. We came to the city of Twells around noon one day and found it uncannily quiet, with black banners flying from its towers. I thought plague was there, and would not go in; but a beggar at the gates said most folks had fled because of the winged beast. We went in only to buy fresh bread and a little more cheese, for Lan had given us some money; then we asked directions to the villages of Crick and Seagrief, and hastened on. We had left the main road, and the way was only a beaten track between fields and alongside woods and streams. After a time we passed no one else at all, save small groups of people fleeing eastward. We asked if they were from Crick or Seagrief, but they said they were not, and could give us no news. They warned us of the dragon, said that doomsday had come, and advised us to turn back. When we went on our way regardless, they shook their heads and called after us that we were mad.

That evening, when I was looking for a sheltered place to sleep, we came upon a burned village. Like Doran it was, and I led the donkey off the road and along the far edges of the burned fields, so we did not have to look upon the destruction. The next day we passed two such villages, and from then on all that we passed were burned. Some were not wholly gone; amid the ruins blackened walls had been mended, and rough thatch laid across. A few survivors lived in them, and came out to tell us to turn back. Some of these villagers had unsightly burns, and their eyes were haunted, without hope.

With every village we passed my terror deepened, and I was certain to my bones that we would never win against the beast that caused all this, no matter how powerful the weapon we had. Always Lizzie appeared calm, and I wondered again if somehow Old Lan had enchanted her, given her some way of flying beyond fear.

So we went on westward, and saw the sea like a steel blade along the edge of the world. Then all the lands were scorched, even the wild moorlands and the grasses by the ash-grey streams. The earth was tinder dry, and a cloud of dust and ash, disturbed by our feet, hung always in the air behind us. As far as the eye could see, the land was burned dry, or covered with a bitter ash. The air smelled foul, our eyes stung constantly, and dead birds and insects lay all about on the parched ground. I suppose they died of starvation, or of the fumes in the air. There were no animals, no rabbits, foxes, hedgehogs, nor anything that moved. The silence was unearthly.

I felt sick most of the time, and our donkey, that until now had been amiable enough, became restive and unruly. I had a hard time keeping it going, and Lizzie said that animals often sensed danger afore humans did. She had seen the bear and wildcat, and Tybalt's horses, all restive as a storm approached, long before the men had wind of it. Having less to eat didn't help our donkey, either; it grazed on the few remaining clumps of grass, though they were thick with ash, and its belly rumbled something terrible. I suppose it felt as ill as I.

There were no trees, and we sheltered that last evening under a wall in one of the burned villages, though it cut into my memories and grieved me sore. Lizzie gave no sign of wariness or fear, excepting that she talked less. That night I became aware of a distant sound, a kind of quiet thundering, that never stopped. Lizzie said it was the sea crashing on cliffs. I thought of St. Alfric's Cove, and could not sleep that night. So I watched over Lizzie as she slept, and murmured to the donkey to keep it calm, and kept a sharp lookout for the dragon. I did not see it.

Dawn came. We ate a little from our dwindling supplies, then I lifted Lizzie onto the donkey. The beast would not move. No matter how much I cajoled or threatened it, it would not move. So I lifted Lizzie down again, and removed the sacks from the donkey's back, and left the beast to roam. We hated leaving it there, shelterless and vulnerable to the dragon, but saw no other way. So we went on, Lizzie clinging to my back as she had when we left Tybalt's, and me carrying the bags of supplies. In the distance stood another village, smaller than the last, and also black and burned. Alone it was, on the cliff at the edge of the world, and I supposed it must be Seagrief.

About midday we came to it. Like the other burned villages, it was deserted, and stank of dragon-fire and death. I did not go inside, nor even look at it. Between the village ruins and the cliff was a little track, which must have been used by the village folk on their way to the beach to go fishing, in the days before the dragon. Still with Lizzie on my back, I followed the track right to the edge of the cliff, where there stood a little tower-like structure, no taller than myself, with a fire pit underneath and holes made in the sides that faced the sea.

"'Tis where they lit the fire to warn the ships," said Lizzie, slipping from my back. Together she and I walked to the end of the track. Dropping the bundles I carried, I gripped Lizzie's arm, and we supported each other as we looked down.

Below our feet the path tumbled crazily down the dizzy cliff, carved into narrow steps and trails that twisted dangerously, sometimes edged with rickety fences for safety, sometimes plummeting through treacherous clefts in the rock. Far below was the wide curve of the cove, contained within the savage cliffs by jagged rocks that marched far out to sea, many of them half hidden by the tide—a fatal trap for unsuspecting ships. The beach was wild and desolate. I could see two fishing boats, abandoned and broken now, and, in the centre of the cove, a tiny shrine built all of stone, with a cross on the top. Beyond it, shining like blue silk, lay the sea. It fair took my breath away, Benedict. Never had I seen the sea; and the hugeness of it, the power of the waves as they crashed across the rocks, the almighty endlessness of it, were awesome to me. When I looked at Lizzie, her face was composed, still, and I guess she was hiding feelings long buried since her childhood. I suppose the ship she came to England on had been wrecked on rocks such as those that stood below.

"We have the right cove, anyway," I said, trying to sound cheerful.

"Keep your voice down, Jude," she warned, whispering. "The dragon may be directly beneath us."

My stomach churned in sudden fear. "Its lair can't be too close to the path," I said, "else the village folk would have discovered it, and destroyed the egg afore it hatched. The cave must be well hidden. Mayhap we won't even be able to find it."

She gave me a knowing sideways look, her lips curved. "Not thinking of giving up already, are you?" she said.

I tried to smile back, though I felt sick. "Me? Give up?" I said.

"You know me better than that, Lizzie."

"Aye, I know you right well," she said.

I looked down the rugged path again, and fought the dizziness that washed over me. It was the only way down; all the rest of the cliff soared sheer to the heavens.

"We'd best hurry down," Lizzie said. "We can hide in the little shrine, and observe the dragon as it comes and goes, and get to know its ways. Then I'll know where and when to lay the fire-dust."

"I don't think I'll be able to carry you down," I said, peering again down the path.

"I know that, dimwit. Give me one of the bags to carry. We'll need one free hand each, to steady ourselves."

"It'll hurt your feet," I said, but she was already picking up the smaller bag, already setting foot on that perilous steep path. Picking up the other bag, I followed her.

I don't know how she managed that track. It was steep and slippery with dust and ash, and we had to watch each place we put our feet, lest we should slip and go plunging to our deaths. Every second I was aware of the beast that lived thereabouts, and after every few steps I cast my glance across the cove and the wide curve of sea and sky, lest it should come winging back. Lizzie must have known, for after a while she whispered, over her shoulder, "It flies only at dawn and dusk, Jude. It will be sleeping now."

"But we might wake it," I whispered back, looking at the cliff opposite. At that moment I lost my footing, and in my wild efforts to clutch the rocks afore I went hurtling into Lizzie, I disturbed a pile of stones. They went clattering and bounding off the precipice down onto the rocks below.

"Aye, you might wake it," said Lizzie, when I was under control again. We were still, listening and looking, but no dragon came. Lizzie added, with a fleeting smile, "But you might not, since its hearing is not good."

Despite her wounded feet and her slowness, she managed better than I, on that terrible path. Mayhap it was something to do with her natural grace, the careful and elegant way of her. Perhaps pain forced her to work out every move afore she made it, so there were no mistakes; perhaps her sense of balance was better than mine. But I felt like a bumbling ox behind her, and often I slipped and slithered, disturbing more stones, certain I sounded like a herd of horses ploughing down the slope. It was awful hot, and I sweated as much from fear as heat, for there was no place to hide if the dragon came.

At last we reached the bottom, and scanned the surrounding cliffs for sign of a cave. There was none.

"Well, that solves our problem," I said, wiping my sleeve across my sweaty face. "The sailors were mistook. Let's rest a bit, then go."

"We can't rest," she said, dragging on my arm. "We must hide in the shrine. Mayhap its cave is in a crevice, seen more easily from the sea than from here. And we must keep our wits about us. We don't know the dragon's habits yet; it may come down to drink, or bathe, during the day."

"Bathe?" I said.

She sighed, long-suffering plain on her face. "Aye, bathe," she said. "Birds do."

"This is hardly a sparrow we've come to kill."

"But it might have a sparrow's inclination to be clean. Make haste!"

I picked up the bundles, and we crossed the pebbly beach to the tiny shrine. I noticed that the pebbles were dark with ash, excepting where the sea had washed over them, and a bitter stench hung about the place.

The shrine was tiny, not half the size of Lan's house, the doorway so small that even Lizzie had to bend her head to get inside. Within, we could stand easily enough, though my head touched the roof. The shrine was stone, save for the timbers laid across for a roof, and covered with turf. The floor was made of smooth pebbles, with a rough fire pit in the centre, its ashes long cold. In one corner lay a pile of rotten furs.

"I suppose St. Alfric slept in these," I said, putting the bundles down and crouching to touch the bedding, hoping that perchance the power of the man might somehow remain, and give me some protection. Then I dropped the stuff, surprised. "There's a blanket here!" I said. "New, by the feel of it. Someone's been here not long past."

"A knight or soldier, doubtless," said Lizzie, "come to slay the beast, and failed."

I looked around for other signs of recent habitation. There was a bag containing mouldy food, but nothing else. All was deep in gloom, for there was but one tiny window facing the sea. Some of the roof had fallen in and a few slender sunbeams slipped through, lighting the rising dust and ash disturbed by our feet.

"I suppose the villagers brought the saint food and fire," I said. "He can't have survived just on the fish the seals brought to him. And it would have been cold as death, in winter."

"'Tis pleasant enough now," Lizzie remarked, looking out the window. "It is the perfect shelter. We can see the dragon come and go, and make our plans."

She went outside again and walked a little way past the shrine, looking at the cliff. I went with her, wanting her to lean on me, to spare her feet. But she would not wait, and I didn't feel inclined to force my help on her. So I followed a step or two behind, carefully, for the ashen stones were slippery. A fresh breeze blew in from the sea, and I would have been glad for its coolness, had it not whipped up that ash, which stung my eyes and tasted bitter in my mouth. Looking along the cliff, I sought the dragon's lair. I hated being out in the open, knowing that mayhap the beast was watching us. Lizzie seemed fearless, gazing up at the towering face of rock as if she searched for nothing more than a buzzard's nest.

"There's no cave," I said. "If there was one, don't you think St. Alfric would have used it, instead of going to all the bother of building a shrine?"

Lizzie said nothing, and I went on, "The men on the ship must have been mistook, Lizzie. There's no cave here. No dragon."

Of a sudden I noticed something lying on the shore not far from me on the water's edge, where the sea had washed the rocks clean. It looked like a bundle of old clothes, or part of a rotten sail from one of the boats. I went nearer. Slowly it dawned on me what the thing was: it was a human corpse, burned black.

I tell you, Benedict, my heart near stopped, for terror. And at that moment Lizzie spoke my name, very low. Tearing my gaze off the mortal remains, I saw her pointing to a place high on the cliff. Looking up, I saw what she had seen. Near the dizzy summit was a blackness, stained all about with ash and soot. From the blackness, hanging partway out, was something lighter coloured. Another corpse.

I crossed myself and said a prayer, and began stumbling to the safety of the shrine, my eyes never leaving that soot-stained lair. "For God's love, Lizzie, come back!" I said.

But a long while she stood there, looking up. When at last she came back, she said, very calm and quiet, "We'll not fail, Jude."

I looked at the slaughtered soldier not far away. There was nothing left of his flesh, nothing to show it was a man, save a sword still clutched in a blackened hand.

"We'll not fail," she said again, taking my arm and turning me away. Together we went back to the shrine. Inside, I felt more trapped than safe.

"We'll be cooked alive in here, if it finds us," I said. "If it even smells us—"

"It won't," she said.

"What of the bodies out there? That one on the beach had a sword still in his hand. It was a soldier, well armed. He would have stayed here. Mayhap the dragon came and dragged him out, and killed him."

"With his sword in his hand?" she said. "He went out to meet it, Jude. He died right bravely."

"He died right stupidly!" I cried, and she hushed me. "Lizzie!" I entreated, quiet, desperate. "We'll never be able to reach that cave. Even Lan, with all her magic, couldn't get up there. The fire-dust is useless, unless we lay it close. All this has been for nought. The quest is over, done. Let's go."

"'Tis barely begun," she said, and sat down and began to unpack the bag with its bundles of fire-dust and the deadly, useless shards.

I sat against a wall and covered my face with my hands. My fingers trembled, and my skin reeked of ash and dragon-fire. The very air stank.

"Tell me you jest," I begged.

"We came to do a work, Jude," she said, "and I'll not go till it is done."

I didn't argue with her, Benedict. There was a boldness about Lizzie, a strength of purpose, that defeated me. Besides, I had made my vow to do all that she said, without argument. But her fervour puzzled me. I remembered that I had sworn nothing about asking questions, and a good one burned on my tongue.

"Tell me another thing, then," I said. "I have a reason to want this dragon dead. Lan wants it dead for reasons all to do with Ambrose. But you: why does it matter to *you*? Why are *you* here, in peril of your life?"

"Because it matters to you," she replied.

"That's no answer."

She bent her head over the bundles of shards, piling them with great care on the little pebbles against the shrine wall, and I could not see her face.

"God's nails and blood!" I said. "You don't know why, do you? Lan's enchanted you—that's why you're here! Isn't it? Isn't it, Lizzie? Why not say it!"

Still she was silent. I swore, and got up and stood in the

doorway, my back to her. "I'm mad to have come here with you," I said angrily. "I'll do as you say, because I vowed I would; but when this quest is done, if we're both alive, I'm taking you to a nunnery to be prayed for and shriven. And I've half a mind to leave you there, after."

We did not speak again for some time, and in the silence my conscience pricked. Whatever else Lizzie might be, bewitched or batty or both, she was exceeding loyal. "I'm sorry," I said. "I did not mean that. 'Twas my fear that spoke. I wanted to make a show of being strong, that is all."

"You *are* strong, Jude," she murmured, "though you know it not."

"More riddles?" I said, trying to sound vexed, though I confess her words softened me somewhat. "You'll drive me from my wits, Lizzie, and then I'll be a lunatic as well as a weakling! Not an ideal nature for a knight about to deal a deathblow to a dragon."

She smiled a little then, and I hoped it meant I was forgiven. We had not smiled much, since leaving Lan's, and I suppose the strain and horror of the last few days had taken its toll on both of us.

And there's another kind of toll—the abbey bells! You must away to prayers, and I to mend some broken walls, afore the wind-month comes. On the morrow, we get to the bit that will make your hair stand on end. Well . . . what hair you have, anyway. Fie! No need to flick ink at me!

SIXTEEN

OOD MORROW, BENEDICT. At least, I suppose it is good. Myself, I cannot rightly tell; we supped with the Abbot again last night, and now my head has a drum in it, and I have a brutal thirst, and my belly threatens any minute to unload itself of all the Abbot's lovely wine. 'Twould be a sinful waste, to be sure, for it's stuff he got in France. Have mercy, Brother—don't bang the ink pot like that! And if I leave this stool in a hurry, don't try to stop me, for 'tis a hellish long way to the lavatorium. Don't laugh, either! I can tell you are, even if you do pretend to look for parchments fallen under your chair; your shoulders shake. 'Tis no laughing matter. I had good reason to drink deep at dinner. Jing-wei was in a strange mood, for a start, and I couldn't say a thing aright. Chen said plenty that pleased her, though. And afterwards she accused me of looking like a grubby peasant—which doubtless I did, compared with the excellent Chen with his silken robes, plaited hair, and pared and polished nails. I'd like to see *him* after mixing clay and straw and dung, to mend tumbledown walls! Anyway, I don't know what she was complaining about; I combed my hair and washed my hands, and got the worst muck off my clothes. 'Tis not my fault I don't have a hundred silken outfits to pick and choose from. Did you know he wears something different every day, including jewels, and every costume is worth a lord's fortune? It's dinner again at the Abbot's table today, and more wonders about China, no doubt. Pray for me if you will, Benedict, for something's going on that unsettles my soul. Something in Jing-wei, that I don't understand. God's bones, man—must you still write down *everything*? I swear, you're as vexing as Jing-wei! I'm getting mortal tired of you starting afore I'm ready! You can throw all this out, for 'tis nought to do with the story, and there's nothing said yet the Abbot doesn't already know. Now start again, another page.

Thank you. Now, to our tale.

St. Alfric's Cove was an ominous, nightmarish place. There were no animals, no birds, only the restless sea sighing and crashing on the rocks, and the overwhelming presence of the beast. It was quiet as a tomb in the shrine, and I felt imprisoned, jittery, half out of my mind for fear, like a man awaiting execution. All that first day I paced, looked constantly out the window, bit my nails, and wished to God that I was anywhere but there. And all the while my thoughts were frenzied, trying to invent a way to get the fire-dust to the dragon. Lizzie was unusually silent, sitting very still with her hands folded in her lap, her eyes half closed.

"We could bring the dragon down here," I said, in a rare moment when my despair lifted a little. "We could prepare the bag of fire-dust and put it on the beach with an animal tied near it, to lure the dragon down. Then, when it breathed on the animal to kill it, it would set the fatal dust alight, and . . ."

Lizzie ignored me. I fell quiet, seeing the holes in my plot. Her serenity was beginning to vex me.

"I hope you're figuring something out," I said, after a while. "I hope you're hatching one hell of a plot, or sprouting wings, or working out a way to fly. Because I'm not exactly thrilled to the veins, stuck in here waiting for something to happen."

Of a sudden her eyes flew open, and she sat up very straight. "Tell me," she said, "is there any wind?"

I stopped my pacing and stuck my head out the window. "Aye," I said. "Coming off the sea. I noticed a breeze before, when we were on the beach. 'Tis stronger now. And blessedly cool."

Slowly, Lizzie stood. Though I warned her against it, she went outside and faced the sea, and lifted her arms to the breeze. Steady and strong, the wind filled her sleeves, billowing them, and tossing her long braids like blue-black banners.

"What are you doing?" I asked crossly, from near the door. "Cooling off, praying, or preparing for flight?"

Lowering her arms, she turned and faced me. She was smiling, half laughing, her face brighter than a new florin from the royal mint. "Flight," she said, and came back into the shrine again.

I followed her, my heart in my boots, thinking she had lost her wits.

"Is this another trick Old Lan taught you?" I asked. "Another bit of witchery?"

"A bit of wisdom," she said, "like the fire-dust. I'm making us a thing that will fly, to take the bag of fire-dust up to the dragon's lair."

"Are you making wings?"

"Be patient. You'll see."

I went and looked out the window at the peaceful sea, and tried to quiet my despair. Behind me, Lizzie delved in one of the bags, and I heard the rustle of her mother's silken dress. There were a few groans as she walked about on the stone floor, and the slithering sound of silk on stones; then I heard the snip of Lan's scissors. I spun around. The silken dress was spread out, scarlet splendour shimmering across near all the floor, and Lan's sewing things were scattered beside it. Lizzie was cutting along one of the seams.

"You're destroying your silk dress?" I cried. "I thought you held it dear!"

"Aye, I do," she said. "But I'm not destroying it; I'm giving it a new purpose, a new form."

"What form? Tell me what you're doing, Lizzie, afore you drive me mad!"

Still with her head bent low as she cut the precious silk, Lizzie said, "In China we fly silk boxes in the wind. I don't know what you would call them in your language; I've never seen them here. We hold them by long cords, and control them from the ground. They are so big and powerful, some of them, that they will lift men into the skies, if the wind is strong. Bowmen use them to fly above enemies hidden in the hills, and shoot the enemies down one at a time. Or soldiers fly in them to spy out enemy land. Sometimes if the silken things are made a certain way, they shriek and howl like devils, and warriors fly them at night over their enemies as they sleep, and the enemies wake and flee, thinking that devils are coming down to destroy them. They are used often in war, like the fire-dust. But they are used in peacetimes, too. My father said he flew in one when he was a youth, high in the mountains, just for the wonder of it."

I was silent awhile, digesting all this. Then I asked, "And you're going to make one so that you can fly up to the dragon's lair on it?"

"No. But I can sew the bag of fire-dust into it, and fly that up to the cave."

"How do you know how to make one? And what's going to set the fire-dust alight, once it's up there?"

"My father made me and my brothers such a flying thing when we were small. I remember it very clearly, for he let me help him make it, and to fly it after. It was a child's toy, not large enough to contain a man. We flew it off the wall that surrounded our city, high over the valleys below. It was a long round tube, not a box, with a bamboo frame inside to hold its shape. When it was filled with wind, flying, it looked like a plump fish, or a dragon. If I can make one the same, the dragon might take it for a foe, and attack it with fire. Then it will set the silk alight, with the bag of fire-dust and shards within."

"God's nails and blood, Lizzie, you're a marvel!" I cried.

"We shall soon see if I am," she said, with a smile that set the blood a-pounding in my veins. "But I cannot take all the praise. I mentioned the flying things to Lan, when I was telling her of my childhood. And when we were packing out provisions, she was very insistent that I bring her sewing things and my mother's silk dress. Mayhap she suspected the dragon's lair might be unreachable, save in this way, and she wanted me to have all that would be necessary. But I still don't have everything, and need your help. Will you find me some fine wood? Thin and light, to make the frame for the silk."

"I might find some back in Seagrief," I said, all eager, making to go right there and then.

But Lizzie said, with that smile again, "Not yet, Jude. 'Tis almost sunset. Go tomorrow. Meanwhile, watch the cave and tell me when the dragon appears."

With hopes soaring, I sat in the entranceway of the shrine and watched the cliff. I could not see the cave from here, for it was hid by a bend in the rock, but I remembered its whereabouts. My eyes never left that place.

The sun sank lower, and it was almost in the sea when Lizzie stopped work and came and sat by me. She brought some bread and cheese and dried figs with her, and gave me some. "Our food is near gone," she said. "In the morning I'll get some sea-food for us. I stayed by the sea with the Gypsies once, and they showed—"

She stopped, and we clutched each other's hands, the food dropped, forgotten. From high in the cliff, drenched in sunset gold, the dragon came. Slowly, almost sleepily, it drifted down. I wanted to retreat back into the shrine, but Lizzie squeezed my arm with her hand, and barely shook her head. "It has bad sight," she whispered, "but movement may give us away."

To my horror, the beast landed on the beach not far from us. It crouched on the pebbles and began cleaning its scales. Like a cat it was, washing itself, only it breathed fire to clean off the dirt, instead of using spit. My heart sank.

"Flame has no effect on it," I said, very low. "Your fire-dust won't work."

"It's not the fire-dust that will do the harm," she whispered back. "But when it bursts into flame it hurls out the shards of flint and steel; those do the harm."

The dragon was meticulous with its cleaning, even burning out the dust between its claws and along its tail. It was beautiful, gleaming like copper in the dying sun. But at times its movements seemed clumsy, and it was much occupied with a place just beneath its left foreleg, to one side of its chest. Then, when it lifted its head to sniff the wind, I saw that in that place was a gaping hole, with blackness oozing out.

"'Tis wounded!" I whispered. "Not mortally, though."

"But it still bleeds," murmured Lizzie. "See how it favours that side? 'Tis not a minor wound, Jude."

She was right; when the beast went down to the sea to drink,

I saw that its movements were not so fluid as before, and it limped badly, for it would not walk upon that leg near the wound. While it drank, its back towards us, Lizzie and I crept slowly into the shrine. Her silken dress lay in pieces along one wall. She leaned on me as we went to the window and cautiously looked out. The beast was in the tide, still drinking the sea. When it was done quenching its thirst, it turned to the corpse on the beach. While we watched, horror-struck, it poured fire across the thing, as if venting fury upon it. It was a wrath terrible to see, and Lizzie and I both turned away.

"It must have been the soldier who gave it the wound," whispered Lizzie. We heard pebbles moving, and every now and then that awful breath, harsh like the winds of hell, and the smell of fire. At last it was over, and there was silence. Lizzie stood and looked out the window. "'Tis flying off," she said. "Along the coast, northward."

Then she came and sat by me again. I had my arms about my knees, and I shook like someone in a fever, stricken with blackest imaginings. After a time I said, "You know, Lizzie, it will do the same to us if it finds us."

"We'll kill it afore then," she said. "It will be a kindness. It must be in fearful agony."

"God's bones—don't tell me you pity it!" I said.

She smiled a little, and picked at a torn fingernail. Lan had pared her nails short, and her hands were little and shapely, like the rest of her. I noticed that her fingers were steady, no tremor at all.

"Are you afraid of nothing?" I asked.

She thought about that awhile, staring out the doorway at

the gathering dusk. At last she sighed and said, "I'm afraid of many things, Jude."

"The dragon, too?"

"Aye. But I don't think on the fear, it only gives it power."

"What do you think on, then? When Lan was about to work on your feet, and you knew you'd be in torment, what did you think on? And when you look at that beast out there, and know we have to kill it, what stops you going half mad with terror? What did you think on, when the dragon came down just now?"

"When Lan worked on my feet, I thought on the joy to come, on walking without pain. It took me beyond the suffering. And you helped more than you know. As for the dragon . . . well, when it came just now, I thought on how lucky we were to have this hiding place, like a shield of stone about us. And I thought on the bag of fire-dust and the shards, and how we shall finish what a soldier began."

"What makes you so sure?"

"Do you remember what Lan said about fear? She said fear was faith in the enemy. If you dwell all the time on what makes you afraid, your own fear sucks the strength out of you. The dragon doesn't make you afraid, Jude—it doesn't even know you live. You make yourself afraid, by believing in the beast's strength, by having faith in it."

I was put in mind again of what Lan said to me about the worst dragons being the ones in my mind. I said, "'Tis hard not to have faith in it, though, when I've seen what it can do."

"Have faith in yourself, too," she said. Leaning close, she pressed her palm flat against my chest, across my heart. "Hold fast to what lies in here," she said. "No one can touch your heart, Jude—not unless you allow them to."

I thought on that closed look she got sometimes, that silent wall she built about herself. I understood it, now. It locked out a multitude of hurts, and locked in a mighty strength. And I despaired, thinking on my own lost dreams and joys, crushed out of me that day I returned to Doran and found it all burned bare. My heart had been touched, all right, with or without my permission—touched and torn, and tossed to utter grief.

I think Lizzie knew what I was thinking, for she said, very gentle, "All things can be made new, Jude."

I looked into her face, and saw such understanding there that I looked away quick, afore she saw my tears. "I think we should finish our meal," I mumbled, scrambling on the stones for the bread and figs that we had dropped when the dragon came. She helped me search, and our hands touched in the dark, and held for two heartbeats. Then we looked for the bread again, and found it. In silence we ate, though the bread was stale and gritty in our mouths.

After, we lay wrapped in our blankets on the stones, listening to the sea, and looking at the stars through the tiny windows. Lizzie slept on the blanket that was already in the place, but I had only stones under me. The wind still blew off the sea, and the air was cool. Moonlight pierced the slits in the roof, for the moon was full, and our tiny shrine seemed filled with misty silver swords. There was a holy power in that place, doubtless from the saint who had once dwelled there.

At some time in the night I woke aching, as if my back had been beaten. I heard Lizzie restless, too.

"I think I prefer a witch's straw mattress to a saint's stones," I said, and she giggled.

"Aye, 'tis uncomfortable and cold," she agreed. "But if you share this place we can sleep on two blankets, which will be softer, and have one to cover us."

Well, I wasn't about to disappoint a maid in distress, so I got up and did as she suggested. It was more comfortable after that, and the smell of mouldy furs was worth the feel of Lizzie warm and close. Don't dip your pen so eager-like in the ink, Brother, for there's nothing thrilling happened, save that I was content for the first time since Doran, and found a wondrous peace in the nearness of a maid. Though I have to confess that in the morning I was sorely tempted, seeing her there against my arm, her hair—

Hark! 'Tis a grand storm outside! Shall I close the window shutters?

There—that's stopped the draft. Still writing? Well, you may as well stop now, for I'll not tell you any more about temptation, 'twill only torture you. I just saw Chen running across the courtyard to the barn, shining wet and all lit up by lightning like one of those bright fire-flowers Jing-wei told me about. He'll be off to make sure the thunder doesn't spook his horse. It's lame, his horse, and he asked the Abbot if he can stay until its hoof is mended. The others are all moving on tomorrow; I suspect he wants to stay on Jing-wei's account. I seem plagued with waiting for hooves to mend. I wish he would leave. His presence here is too disturbing. I confess, though, that Chen is making me think on things I have not thought about before. I've been remembering Old Lan of late, and the wisdom she had. I'm thinking now that mayhap she was no witch at all, but just a woman with more knowledge than perhaps we are comfortable with. Mayhap wisdom like Lan's is only another side of truth, if truth be like a gem, cut on several sides to let the full light through. I see that sideways look, Brother. I'm sorry; I'm merely trotting out my thoughts. For God's love, don't write this down! I might be burned for heresy!

SEVENTEEN

ON'T LOOK SO CAUTIOUS, Brother—I'll not bite off your head today. I'm sorry for my ill humour yesterday, and some of the things I said. They were not meant, and were certainly not deserved, after all your kindnesses to me. And you are doing well with all your writing: the Abbot told me that he read what you've done so far, and he likes it very well. He also likes the bits about the monastery, for they record a part of history as well, so he says. I suspect, between you and me, that he rather likes the idea of having his own name in a book. So you'd better write it: Abbot Dominic, of the Monastery of St. Edmund at Minstan, in the year of our Lord 1356. Perchance he'll be famous one day, for he's doing a newfangled thing: he's building a school for ordinary folks, so they can learn to read and write. Learning shouldn't be only for the rich, he said. And he's started a goose farm for the quills, to keep your writing brothers well supplied. He's offered me paid work looking after the geese, and I'm thinking on it, for it sounds a pleasant way of life. He offered Jing-wei work, too. He's most impressed with the fact that she can read and write in her own language, and has offered to teach her to read and write in English, if she will afterwards become a teacher in his school. However, she won't say if she will or no. She is quiet these days, and I think that, for some reason beyond me, I have offended her. She spends much of her spare time with Chen. But enough of my woes . . .

I woke at dawn the next day, and lay listening to the strange breathing of the sea as it came and went upon the beach. I would have stayed long abed, for it was pleasant there with Lizzie, but she leaped up right quick once she woke, to watch for the dragon's return. Well after sunup it came, flying low and with its belly full. It went straight to its cave, and we did not see it again all day.

All morning Lizzie worked on the cut pieces of her mother's dress, sewing them with Lan's needle and threads into a long silken sheath. Right cunningly she sewed, and quick. I helped when I could, holding the pieces of silk together so the seams stayed true while she stitched.

Near the middle of the day we drank the last of our water. Lizzie asked me to carry her down to the shore when the tide went out, and I watched as she upturned rocks at the water's edge. She stood up, smiling, with a devilish-looking creature caught between her forefinger and thumb. She said it was a crab, good to eat. I gave her my knife, and she dealt swiftly with it, pulling off its claws and sucking the flesh from them. "The Gypsies ate these," she said. "There are other sea-foods, too, if we can find them. Most are fine uncooked."

She offered me one of the creature's evil-looking claws, but I shook my head, the bile rising in my throat. Truth to tell, I felt constantly sick in that place. I think it was the smell of it, the bitter air, the knowing that we were in our enemy's domain. I shook in fear the whole time we were out there, while Lizzie hunted for her grotesque food.

Back in the shrine, Lizzie began to sew again. She was making a long sleeve-like thing, and I couldn't for the life of me see its resemblance to a fish or a dragon. Trusting her, I said nothing, save that I would go to Seagrief that afternoon to look for the sticks she needed.

"This will be ready by the time you get back," she said. "I'll slide the sticks where they need to go, and we can fly it tonight."

"Tonight?" I cried, alarmed. "So soon?"

"Just to see if it works," she said, with her lips curved. "Nothing to get ruffled about. The dragon will be safely gone while we try it."

"I'm scared, all the same," I confessed. "All the time I'm scared, in this place. I've tried to have faith in myself, Lizzie, but I can't. I keep seeing the dragon, and Doran."

"Why are you afraid at this moment?" she asked.

"The dragon might fly out of its cave. It might come here and burn us out. Do to us what it did to that soldier out there."

"Aye. And a shipload of mad pirates might land in the cove, and cut us to pieces. Or the stars might fall, or you might tumble down and break your stupid neck, or—"

"'Tis not funny, Lizzie!"

"I'm not jesting!" she said, standing up. "Is it likely that the dragon will fly down here in broad daylight, just to sniff inside this shrine?"

"No," I said, doubtfully. "I suppose not."

"Then what are you afraid of? I'm busy with my sewing. The dragon's asleep in its lair. You're standing safe and sound inside a stone shelter. What's to be afraid of?"

I sighed, and half smiled at her. "Only an angry maid," I said.

Picking up one of our bags, she emptied it of all save our two water skins. "Fill these while you're in Seagrief," she said. "And make sure you collect sticks that are light and strong. Willow, if you can find it, for it will bend without breaking."

"I think everything will be scorched dry," I said, taking the bag, "but I'll do my best."

"I have no doubt you will," she said, and to my surprise reached up to kiss my cheek. "Take care," she added. "I need you, Jude of Doran."

My heart sang all the way up the cliff path, and even the burned walls of Seagrief couldn't cool my joy. I found the well, lowered the bucket, and filled our water skins. The water was grey with ash, for the little roof over the well had burned and fallen in, but it didn't taste too foul. I drank deeply there, then went to look for the sticks Lizzie needed.

It was terrible to rummage about in those devastated homes, searching strangers' sorry rubble. I found several blades from knives, and though the handles were burned away and the steel was black, they were still sharp. I wrapped them in a scrap of scorched leather, to take back for Lizzie to put in the fire-dust with the flint and metal shards. I found other things as well, too terrible to talk about. Twice I near spewed, and I ached, thinking on Doran. I felt displaced, unreal, like a lost phantom poking about in some forgotten part of hell. It was strange to look up at blue skies and realise that the rest of the world was still there, sound and ordinary in parts.

At last I discovered pieces of a wattle fence behind a blackened clay wall, and some of the willow sticks were undamaged by the fire. I pulled them out, and found them still supple; the fence must have been built just afore the dragon came. I got all the sticks that were available, binding them into a bundle that I could carry on my back, and returned to the beach.

Partway down the cliff path I stopped to rest, and looked to where the lair was. In a moment of pure, mad defiance, I lifted my right hand and jabbed two fingers in the air. "I've still got my bow fingers, you old lizard!" I yelled, and the words echoed around the cove like an abbey bell. Then I scrambled down the path and raced to the shrine. But that small act of boldness had done my soul good.

When Lizzie saw me, she laughed. "I heard your battle cry," she said. "The dragon must be mortal scared."

"Aye," I replied, smiling, handing her a swollen water skin. "Only it's not my fingers it needs to worry about, but yours, as you do that sewing there."

"It's done," she said, "and needs only the sticks to give it shape, to hold it open so the wind can fill it."

"'Tis wondrous work, Jing-wei," I said.

She looked at me strangely, a smile playing about her lips. "You called me by my true name," she said.

I was flustered a moment or two, because of the pleasure on her face. "Well, it fits you better than Lizzie," I said. "Besides, only a brave maid from Hangchow could sew a silken flying-thing, and use it to slay a dragon."

She lifted the water skin to her lips, but not before I saw the red blush on her cheeks. I swore to myself that I would never again call her by any name save her own true one.

As she drank, I dropped the sticks on the floor beside her, and unbound them. "There was little left," I said. "I got these from a fence that had been only partly burned. They're supple, still."

Marvelling, I watched as she slid the sticks down some of the seams she had sewn, then stitched the silk around the frame to make it stable. She gave me two of the longer, more supple sticks and asked me to soak them in the sea, to make them softer. I did as she said, all the while keeping a wary eye on the lair above. Back in the shrine, I watched as Jing-wei slid the wet wands into the wider end, curving them into a hoop, binding them into place within the silk. Then she spread her work along the floor. Like a long hollow snake it was, wide at the end supported and held open by the willow frame, and tapering to several silken tails. The main body of the thing stretched the full length of the shrine; the tails were as long again. For size and colour, I suppose a half-blind dragon might perceive it as a fledgling of its kind, though a fatally deflated one.

Jing-wei saw my doubt, and smiled. "It will come alive in the wind," she assured me. Then she took one of the balls of cord Lan had given her, cut off several lengths, and fixed them to the silken sleeve, near the willow hoops at the wide end. One of the cords she did not cut, but left attached to the ball. "With this we'll control the silk dragon, even when it's far in the sky," she said. "Don't look so forlorn, Jude; I know what I'm about."

I went and leaned on the window ledge, looking at the sea. The wind still came in, strong and steady, and I did not ask what she would do if that night the air was still.

"I have another task for you," she said, from behind me. "Will you go out and fetch that sword you saw? We'll need it, if the beast is only wounded."

I turned to face her. She was bent over the ashes on the floor, mixing water into them with a stick.

"Lan said our weapon cannot fail," I said.

"Aye, so she did. And it won't. The beast will be torn apart. But it might not die at once, and I will not leave it suffering. Please fetch the sword."

"His hand was still about the hilt," I said, faltering. "I don't . . . I'm not . . ."

She said nothing, but dipped one end of a willow stick into the sooty paste. Then carefully she began painting eyes on the silken thing she had made, near the larger end.

Full of dread, I went out to do as I was told. But the corpse was gone, dragged out by the waning tide, or burned to nothingness by the beast. I found a strip of leather, metal-studded, caught between the rocks, and knew it was the soldier's belt. It seemed familiar, with those studded bits, and I supposed I had seen another like it in a different place. The sword I found at last, black as the stones it lay among, half buried in sand. I was afraid to touch it, lest some part of the dead soldier's flesh still clung to it, with dragon's blood; but it was clean save for the soot that covered it. I scoured it with sand, taking off most of the blackness, then lifted it by the hilt, feeling its awful weight, and raised the blade to the sky.

Again a strange memory stirred in me, and I stared hard at the handle, the fine work etched along the blade. Then it hit me:

this sword was Tybalt's! And the moment I knew that, there crowded into my head a dozen other things: the image of Richard that night the minstrel told us where the dragon was, and how Richard's face had shone, as if he heard a summons; words Richard had spoke, and how he longed to slay a dragon the way his forefathers had; how the soldier here upon the beach had worn no armour, no helmet, and had only this sword. And the studded belt I had seen abandoned in the rocks—it was the belt Richard had worn. I remembered, too, another thing, so awesome and powerful that I scarce could take it in: I remembered that the soothsayer had told Richard that this sword—this sword I held now in my hands—would be the sword to slay the last dragon.

I cannot tell the feeling I had as I stood there on the beach that moment, with that sword held high, and in my mind and heart a sense so strong of destiny before me, and a thousand souls behind me, like angel-guards gathered about, and saints, and all the company of heaven, to help me do this thing that was ordained for me. I thought on what Old Lan had said about my destiny, and how Jing-wei and I were bound by fate to find her place; and I thought on the sword and its history, and how all things had come together here, on this ashen shore, with a strange weapon only Jing-wei understood, and this star-fated sword, and a dragon to be slain. And I swear, Brother Benedict, there was then no fear in me, no doubt, but only a sense of destiny, and a steel-strong will to win.

I felt Jing-wei beside me, and lowered the sword point to the stones, for my arms were mortal tired.

"'Tis a long while you've been out here, Jude," she said. "The sun is going down. Come back to the shrine, afore the dragon flies."

"This is Tybalt's sword," I said.

She limped a little way past me, looking to where the body had been, her hand shading her eyes from the low sun. "Then Tybalt should be buried," she said, very low. "At least, a pile of stones should be raised over him, and a cross placed where he lies."

"The body's gone," I said. "And it wasn't Tybalt. It was Richard. I saw his belt caught in the rocks, the studded belt he wore."

She went very quiet, thinking; then she said, with a look almost of relief: "I didn't kill him, then, that night in the forest."

There was a movement high in the sun-gold cliff; we looked up to see the dragon emerge, slow, from its lair. It stopped in the entrance, only its head and neck visible to us. Seemingly unaware of us, it looked out to sea.

"Don't move," warned Jing-wei.

"I wasn't about to," I said, visions still blazing in my head. "Let it come down here now, if it will, and I'll do battle with it."

But it flew away, not even coming down to drink. Straight towards the sun it went, barely moving its wings, gliding in the golden wind; then it turned and flew inland, and was lost in the twilight skies beyond the cliff.

When I went back to the shrine Jing-wei was already gathering up the silken dragon she had made. I noticed that she had placed a little willow raft within the sleeve, fixed to the sticks along the seams, and the leather bag of fire-dust was sewn firmly onto it. A long twist of silk emerged from the bag, and I asked her what it was for.

"It will catch alight before the leather does, and take the fire straight to the heart of the dust. Then it will blow apart, flinging out the metal shards and the sharp flints."

"I brought back some knives from Seagrief, too," I said, putting down the sword, and helping her.

"I found them. All are inside, carefully placed. I've been busy while you were out there dreaming."

"You remember what Richard's seer said about the sword, don't you?"

She smiled at me across the shining length of silk, plum-red in the purple dusk. "Aye, I remember," she said. "But don't let dreams replace your wits, Jude. You need both. That was Richard's trouble; he had visions, but lacked knowledge."

Down to the sand we went. The tide had been sucked out towards the world's end, leaving fatal rocks exposed, their jagged points black against the sun's last light. Between the rocks, where the sea had withdrawn, lay long stretches of wet sand.

Out on that shining sand, with the wind to our backs, Jing-wei and I faced the towering cliff and the dragon's cave. She gave me the silken sleeve to hold, telling me to raise it high, the open end towards the wind. The silk streamed from my hands, tugging with the force of the breeze, and Jing-wei held the ball of cord still attached to it.

"Let it go!" she cried.

I did. Of a sudden, like a child's strange toy leaping into life, the scarlet silk writhed and unfurled, swelling with the wind, blossoming, bursting into shape. Like a living thing it rose, leaping in the warm wind that swept up the face of the cliff. Higher and higher it rose, tugging and tossing, bright as fire against the first stars. Oh, Benedict, it was grand! Never have I seen such a fine thing made by human hands! As I watched Jing-wei feeding it more cord, letting it fly higher, freer, I thought of what she had said about her father standing in such a contraption, being flown like a falcon above hills and valleys, beyond earth and trees, and I longed to do the same.

So enthralled I was, I almost forgot the purpose of our task. But Jing-wei had not: she flew the silk high near the dragon's lair, holding it there by the cord, watching as it rose and dipped in the growing dark.

"'Tis magic!" I breathed.

"Nay, 'tis no more cunning than a windmill's blades, or the sails of a ship," she said. "It is only a thing harnessing the wind."

"So if the wind drops, all is lost?" I asked.

"Nay, but we would have to try again another time," she said. "But it's flying well now, and the wind is strong. If I bring it down it may be damaged on the stones. We'll leave it where it is, to wait for morning, and the dragon."

And that is what we did. She placed the ball of cord on the beach, and weighted it down with a rock. Then she got more crabs to eat, which I shared this time, out of my stomach's dire need, and we sat with our backs against the little shrine, to wait. Close at hand, gleaming in the moonlight, lay Tybalt's fateful sword. And all the while the silken dragon soared outside the lair, splendid and defiant, with its cargo of spiked death.

And that, Brother, is a splendid note on which to end this day's work!

EIGhTEEN

LL READY AND WAITING, Brother Benedict? I warned you our tale was hotting up. Which is more than I can say for your monastery. Doesn't the Abbot believe in comfort? I've been peeling onions in the kitchen all morning, just to be near a fire. I'm glad you have one here—do you mind if I pile on a bit more wood? The rain's settled in for good, along with the noble Chen. I think he's addling Jing-wei's wits. Yesterday she asked me if I still thought of her as a freak. She asked other things, too, which wounded me to my soul. I mean, I think so highly of her, it hurts to think I might have done things to make her believe otherwise. I asked her if I had done somewhat to offend her, and she said it wasn't what I'd done that distressed her, but what I hadn't done. And that was all she'd say. I really can't fathom her out, Brother. And you're the wrong man to help me, being a monk, and blissfully removed from all these difficulties. I tell you, I'm seriously considering becoming a monk myself, just to find some peace. I could swear obedience to Abbot Dominic, for I like him greatly; the vow of poverty wouldn't alter my life at all, and neither would the vow of chastity, the way I'm going. Sorry. I've made you blush again. Back to my tale, to the safer territory of dragons.

That night I kept watch while Jing-wei slept, her head against my shoulder. Of a sudden I realised that the silken sheath had shifted, was lower than before, and dangerously close to the cliff. I could see it clearly in the full moonlight, the colour of blood, spiralling crazily almost against the cliff, its shadow flapping like a tortured thing on the silvered stone. I woke Jing-wei, and she stumbled to her feet, crying, "The cord! Wind in the cord!"

I ran ahead of her to the place where the ball lay under the stones, found it at last in the shallow water, and wound frantically. "Run backwards!" Jing-wei screamed. "Get it away from the cliff!"

I did as she said, though the tide was coming in again, and waves crashed about my legs. The cord tugged in my hands, and afore long I felt the pull grow steady and strong as wind filled the silk, lifting it, and I saw it rise free and powerful again, away from the cliff. It was up near the dragon's lair when Jing-wei got to me. We both were thigh-deep in the waves.

"Well, it's flying true again," I said, full of relief.

"Aye, you did well," said Jing-wei. I grinned, looking at our gorgeous trap. And then I saw another thing: a blackness that flew against the stars, blocking out their light. A glimmering like faded gold, and a breath of fire.

"Jesus' wounds—the dragon's back!" I cried.

I tried to run towards the shrine, the ball of cord still in my hands, but Jing-wei flung herself at me, pushing me back. "Stay here!" she cried. "Fly the silk!"

The dragon had seen us. In horror I watched as, ignoring our trap, it turned instead to the shore, to the place where we stood in the tide. I watched it descend, and it seemed that all time stopped, transfixed with the beast that drifted, deathly slow, between earth and heaven. I was aware of the way its belly glowed brighter then faded as it breathed, and of the beauty of the stars beyond; was aware of the wild, clean coldness of the wind, and the warmth of Jing-wei's hands about my arm; and thought, in those uncanny moments, of my family waiting for me in heaven, perhaps not very far off.

And then the dragon was directly overhead, dropping fast— so fast!—towards us, its breath harsh and hissing. Fire poured through the night above our heads. Dragging Jing-wei with me, I dived into the tide. The barbed tail whipped the air just above my head. I heard the whistle of wind across taut wings, that awful outpoured breath, the hiss of flame on water. I felt Jing-wei floundering beside me, and caught her close. Waves crashed over us; fire and water mixed, the smell of burning and taste of salt. Praying, sobbing, I grabbed for the lost cord, found it wrapped about my wrist. Then fire again, and the cold force of the sea. Fighting for air, coming up through churning sand and sea, I saw the dragon spiral upwards, felt the rush of wind and fire and foam, glimpsed water drops aflame.

Then another wave broke across us. Still holding Jing-wei, I staggered to my feet. My eyes stung with salt and sand; I scarce could see. At last I got my breath, and we both looked up, saw the scarlet silk still flying, and the silver brightness of the stars.

But the dragon was gone.

Cursing, I helped Jing-wei up onto the dry sand. The tide tugged at us; our clothes were filled with sand and sea, heavy, dragging. Still holding the cord, I searched the skies, the shadowy cliffs, the long stretch of ashen shore. But the beast was gone, vanished. I thought of the time at Lan's when it had disappeared behind her house, and then come back again, silent as a leaf afloat on wind. Was it just above the cliff, drifting, waiting to swoop down in final attack?

"Sweet Jesus, 'tis playing with us!" I cried, panic-stricken.

Jing-wei took the cord of the flying silk, unwinding the tangle from my wrist. My eyes never left the skies, but I could feel her fingers cold and trembling on my skin. I was trembling myself, so much that my teeth clattered.

"It has not the brains for playing hide-and-seek," she said, very low and sounding calm, though her voice was not quite steady. "It is gone, frightened off for a time. It can't be in its lair; it would have set the fire-dust alight."

"It'll be back, make no doubt," I said. "The skies grow light already; it will come again, with the day."

I discovered, then, that speaking hurt my lips. They were burned, not badly, but as they sometimes were when I worked all day in the summer fields. I looked more closely at Jing-wei. In the growing light I saw that she, too, was burned a little. But she must have turned her face away from the dragon's blast, for only one ear was scorched, a part of her right cheek, and the edges of her hair. I realised that we had been saved by the sea, when the dragon poured its fire on us.

Mayhap Jing-wei was thinking the same thing, for she said,

grateful-like, "Fate is on our side, Jude. We have another chance. 'Tis more than most have, who take on dragons."

She looked up to check that the silk still flew aright, then placed the ball of cord beneath a stone again, to hold it firm. Her movements were slow, for she was hampered by wet skirts. Then, telling me to keep watch—as if I needed telling!—she went into the shrine, and came out with a pot of Lan's ointment for our burns. "I'll anoint our war wounds," she said, with a brief smile. "And after, if the beast is still not back, we'll find some breakfast, for I'm mortal hungry after our first battle."

"'Twas hardly a battle," I said. "A botch-up, more like."

She shot me a disapproving look, and began spreading Lan's potion on my scorched face.

While we were anointing our burns, the wind began to drop. The silken sheath dipped low and flapped against the cliff, so I helped Jing-wei bring it down. We laid it carefully in the shrine, to wait until the wind's return. The sun came up, and still the dragon did not return. As the day grew hot, we spread our outer clothes to dry on the sand beside the shrine. I could not help thinking on the strangeness of it—me, bashful Jude of Doran, on a lone shore with a lone maid, and both of us in our underthings. And nought exciting happening, excepting that any moment we might be attacked by a dragon.

With great caution, still scanning the skies, we went down to the shore and hunted crabs and the strange sea-creatures in their spiral shells. I was not hungry, but Jing-wei ate hungrily enough, while I kept lookout. I was in a sweat, I don't mind confessing, mortal scared in case the beast returned and found us unprepared; but in the early afternoon the wind came in, constant as before, and we flew the snare again. And again we tied the end of the cord to a large stone, so we could take shelter and yet leave the silken trap in place.

Then we pulled on our dry outer clothes and sat in the sun with our backs to the shrine, and kept watch for the dragon.

All afternoon we waited. And all the time my fears grew, for it was not the dragon's habit to be away all day. Disturbed, had it changed its tactics, grown cunning and more deadly still? I did not voice my fears, but sat with my hand on the sword, my eyes scouring the skies, the restless sea, the savage cliffs. And near that deadly place at the top of the cliffs, bloodred in the sun, soared the silken snare, serene and strong, waiting, waiting.

Then, an hour before sundown, we spied the dragon—a small spot in the northwest skies. Without a word, Jing-wei and I both stood and went into the shrine. I stood behind her, looking over her head, as we watched from the tiny window. We did not speak, but we both knew that if the dragon came down first to the beach, as it had before, then these moments might be our last. I put my arms about her, and she covered my hands with her own, and held tight.

To our horror, the dragon did come down to the beach. But it went only to the sea, and spent a long time drinking. It stayed there in the shallow waves, cleaning itself, and I noticed that its limp was worse than before, and once it tore at its wound with its horned snout, as if it were trying to tear away the pain. Then it left the sea and turned towards us. My heart near stopped, and I felt Jing-wei grow taut within my arms. But the beast lingered on the foaming edge of the tide, sniffing at some low rocks and clumps of dark seaweed. It licked them with its forked tongue, tore at them with its horn, then breathed fire on them. I wondered whether, with its poor eyesight, it thought the rocks and weed were Jing-wei and me. Mayhap it had taken us for sea-creatures, and did not connect us with the shrine and human foe. The tide had come in again, covering our footprints and the smell of us, and though the dragon was long examining those rocks and lumps of weed, it came no nearer to our hiding place.

At last it lifted its wings to the wind, and leaped upwards. Water streamed from its limbs, and its bright scales shone like gems in the evening light. Again it struck me how beautiful it was, how graceful and shining and strong. Almost lazily, it soared towards its lair.

I thought at first the dragon had not seen the silk, for it seemed quite unconcerned; then of a sudden it gave a peculiar, raucous cry and spread its wings to slow its flight. It drifted back and forth along the cliff, its long neck outstretched towards the snare. It seemed unsure, cautious; then it began wheeling about the silk like a bird about its prey. I hardly breathed, for expectation and fear, and Jing-wei whispered something in her own language—a prayer, mayhap.

Then I saw that the dragon must have got entangled in the cord, for the silken sheath tossed violently, and the beast's flight became fitful. It veered and turned, all the time uttering its rough and dreadful cries; then it darted at the silk and shot a breath of fire. The silk flashed, caught the flame, danced, writhed like a living thing ablaze. And then the fire-dust caught alight.

Radiance leaped across the skies, along the cliff, the brilliant beach, the bright dragon. Then came the sound, booming like thunder from hell itself. The very earth groaned; I heard a roaring and cracking, and the cliff began to slide. Slow it was, as I remember it: half the world collapsing in a cloud of sunlit dust; the scent of the fire-dust; the vast blackness falling, falling; and, sinking with it, the dragon, tumbling over and over, fire and light, flame and dust, beautiful even in death. And all around rained shards of rock, and dust, and bits of stone.

A long time the rumbling continued, perilously close. Crouching down, I sheltered Jing-wei with my body, while stones and earth rained down upon the shrine. Dust poured in through the windows and door and through the cracks in the roof, and once a rock thrice the size of my head crashed through, splintering the roof and missing us by a hand's breadth. At last the dust settled and all was quiet outside. Trembling, Jing-wei and I stood and crept out onto the shore.

There was hardly any beach remaining. Half the cliff had sunk into the sea, and at the top, vivid against the sunset skies, were the remains of some of the houses of Seagrief. Others had fallen, and I could see the burned timber and roof beams sticking like bones out of the rubble. That part of the cliff with the pathway had survived intact, along with St. Alfric's shrine. All else was gone, tumbled down in a chaos of shattered rock and broken earth. On a slab of jagged rock hung a strip of tattered scarlet silk. It fluttered in the wind, bright like a banner on a battleground. And nearby, tarnished and unmoving, lay the dragon.

"I won't need the sword," I said. And I remember feeling disappointed a little, for the prophecy had been wrong.

Jing-wei was looking across the shattered rocks at the dragon. "Get the sword," she said, and I caught alarm in her tone.

Full of dread, I looked again to where the dragon lay. Its head was raised, waving about on that long neck as if it were a flower too heavy for its stem. Groaning, screaming, the dragon breathed fire. Then it tried to lift itself on its front legs, but failed.

Feeling in a dream, I got the sword and faced the pile of rubble where the dragon lay. It was ten paces or so from me, lying still again, its breaths long and terrible. With each breath it shot out fire, but the flames were greenish-coloured, weak. The air stank, bitter and scalding to my throat. I lifted the sword to the bloodred skies.

"Jesus help me," I said, and began climbing the stones.

The dragon's head was stretched towards me, though resting on the ground. As I walked higher, I saw the bulk of its body, twisted, awkward, its belly and throat lacerated by the razor-edged metal blades and shards embedded in it. Where the scales were shattered and the flesh wounded, black slime ran out. The wings, once so luminous and fine, were mangled. In defeat the creature looked deflated, drab, its inner fire dying. Its damaged tail twitched and flickered, the broken barbs rasping on the rocks. The creature watched me approach, its head side-on to me. I could see only one eye; it was a ball of molten gold, the iris long and black and slitted, like a cat's in the daylight. It blinked, a second skin sliding momentarily across the gold. I remembered what Lan had said about the dragon seeing best from the side, and knew it was aware of my every move.

I went nearer, the sword raised high. I wish I could say that at that moment I felt again what I had felt when I first held the sword on that shore, when I knew I stood in glorious company, protected and empowered by destiny. But at that moment, when I stood before the dragon face-to-face, within a breath of fire and hell and death, I felt nought save grim terror, and could not move to save myself, nor swing the sword, nor breathe. I swear even the blood stopped in my veins. The dragon must have known it, for it lifted its head, its eye still blazing on me, and raised itself on its front legs. Slowly, it dragged itself around to face me straight on. Held in a terrible mastery, I could not move; I could see both its eyes, saw its mouth open, the black tongue flick towards me. Then I heard it draw in a long last breath, gathering force for one final, fatal onslaught of killing fire. It was then, betwixt that breath and its release, I remembered who I was and all that stood behind me, and I closed my eyes and swung down the sword.

I felt the blade hit flesh and bone and stone. The force of the blow tore through my hands and up my arms, shattering me, smashing me, as if the fire-dust itself had burst within, and blown apart my heart. At the same instant heat poured over me. I thought I heard a great bell toll, and that death had come. There was a huge sense of surrender, and sorrow, and a profound relief. Then I realised that the bell was only the ringing of the sword on stone, that I was still on my feet, the hilt of the sword still clenched in my hands. I tried to open my eyes, but could not. Panicking, blind, I dropped the sword and staggered on the stones. I was sobbing, I think, or screaming; there was a cry from somewhere, echoing around the cove. Then I felt a hand on my arm, and something beating on my clothes.

"All's well—'tis dead," said Jing-wei. "You killed it." But she sounded worried, and my panic deepened. Why could I not see?

"What's wrong?" I cried, and my lips felt thick, more puffed up and painful than before. "What happened?"

She did not reply, but dragged me along the stones, down-wards. Stumbling, I gripped her sleeve, felt her shaking. I could smell my clothes smouldering. Then there was water all around, and she was making me kneel in it, splashing the cold sea across my face and chest, my hands, my clothes. It was then the pain came, and I knew.

"Am I burned very bad?" I asked, half sobbing.

She helped me stand. The waves still washed about our legs, and I gripped her arms to steady myself. Even my palms were burned, for I suppose the sword too had been heated instantly by that blast. Faintness came over me. I heard her say, with her usual calm, "Your skin's red, like a child's when it's been in the sun too long. Your eyelashes are gone, and your brows. The lids are puffed, but it's only the outside skin where the lashes burned. When the swelling goes you'll see again. I'll mend your burns with the potions Lan gave to us. You'll be fine, Jude. 'Tis all only skin-deep. The dragon's fire was much weakened, and your clothes protected most of you."

I put my hands to my face, and removed them fast. I felt my hair; it was frizzed all over, burned short. "Like the time Tybalt played his sword about me," I said, and tried to laugh. The laugh hurt, stretched my skin too tight.

"Aye. You have a wild time, getting shorn," Jing-wei said. Her voice was broken, changed by laughter or tears, or both; and I reached out for her and pulled her close. Then we both wept, I think, from relief and nerves stretched too far, and awe at the thing that we had done.

The next hours blur in my memory. Jing-wei took me back to the shrine and anointed my scorched skin with oil and ointments.

I remember thirst and pain, and the terror of not being able to see. A dozen times I made Jing-wei go and look outside, in case the dragon was still alive and crawling here to kill us. Then I slept, I think, or fainted.

When I came to, I heard a pounding sound outside, like stones being thrown, and staggered blindly to where I thought the door might be. I found it at last. Sunlight fell warm on me, and I realised it was morning. I called to Jing-wei.

"I'm covering the dragon!" she called back.

A while later she came to the shrine, and put into my hands a smooth disc-like object, larger than my outspread hand. "One of its scales," she told me. "'Tis a beautiful thing, Jude. Clear like ice on a winter pond, but the colour of polished copper. And there are colours layered within it, purples and greens and blues. It's a changing thing, more lovely than a jewel."

"And more rare than one," I said.

I felt her hand on mine; our fingers linked.

"I placed Tybalt's sword in the pile of stones," she told me. "I stood it upright, hilt skyward, like a cross."

I thought it seemed a fitting monument, since Richard used it, too, and began the work we finished. It was a memorial to him as well, for he had courage, despite his faults. I wanted to tell Jing-wei how well she had done, but my lips hurt. I said instead: "I'm mortal tired, Jing-wei."

And that, Brother Benedict, is how I felt after killing the last dragon. Tired, and triumphant, and dazed with disbelief. There was astonishment, too, that it was over so quick. Old Lan had been right—the worst of it had been the haunting fear, the dragon in my own mind, that had roasted me slow with its fire and tortured me for days and weeks on end, over and over again, in my dreams and dark imaginings. The real fight, when it came, had been over in moments.

That first day after felt unreal, like a dream. For most of it I slept, and in my dreams heard the sliding of silk, like scales slithering, and smelled fire. When I woke Jing-wei was burning something out on the beach. Her little silk shoes, she told me afterward, and the rest of her mother's dress, save for the fragment where her mother had embroidered her name in Chinese. She has it still. And we have the dragon's scale, though no one has seen it save ourselves. I want to do something special with it, so it will not be lost. I thought perhaps when you've finished our book you might like to set the scale within the leather cover, perhaps etch a dragon on it, since your artwork is so fine.

And talking of your artwork, I do admire the letters you've done at the beginning of each day's work. You've been a good listener, Benedict, and a most excellent scribe. But I think now I need a break. A walk in the cloisters, perhaps, to breathe in the fresh air, and smell the rain in the herb garden. I've been thinking more and more on staying here and becoming a novice, for I've grown passing fond of this place and its peace.

Well, I'll be off, and see you on the morrow, for the ending to my story.

NINETEEN

OOD MORROW, Brother! Well, truth to tell, 'tis not so good. There's a sorrow in my heart today, and I know not why. Chen has asked Jing-wei to marry him. I ought to be glad for her sake. This was what I'd hoped for her—that she'd find someone from her own country, and be happy with him. And now it's happening, and I am come to grief. She's not too glad herself, and I don't know why. She told me that in China 'tis a disgrace for a bride to have big feet and marriages are made, or unmade, on whether feet are bound. In the wedding ceremony the groom's kin check the bride's feet for smallness. She's trapped between two worlds, she says, and I have a strange feeling that she blames me for it. Or she wants something from me, and I don't know what it is. What should I do? You know me well by now and must have some wisdom you can offer. No—don't write your answer down, I can't read. Whisper to me.

What?

Marry her? *Marry her?*

Corpus bones—what kind of advice is that, from a monk? I'm mortal shocked, dumbstruck, speechless. Well, not quite speechless. You ought to be ashamed of yourself, Brother Benedict, for having such a mad notion in your head. How could I marry her? I have nothing, while Chen has everything—wealth, beauty, good prospects, a nobleman's house and land in China. What could I offer her? Work on a goose farm, and sweet little else, save for what we already have—our friendship and trust, the easiness in each other's company, the—

You smile, Benedict.

God help me, you're mad, or I am, or we both are. But I'm off to see Jing-wei. And here's a kiss for your advice—one on your forehead, there—and one on each of your lovely cheeks. Look— you've smudged your ink and spoiled the page. Serves you right—you shouldn't be writing all this, anyway. I'll come again afore the lighting of the lamps, and let you know how I get on. Meanwhile, say a prayer for me!

Benedict! I have sweet news! But I'm not allowed to tell it, for Jing-wei wants to come and tell you herself. So I'll just sit down here upon my stool, and calm my frantic heart, and let God know of my gratitude, and get on with the ending to my tale.

There's not much more to tell. Ah—here's Jing-wei already, to tell the news! I swear, she must run near as fast as I do, these days!

Here's a stool for you to sit on, dear heart. And don't mind that Benedict still writes; he records everything, and I suppose that what you have to say now is also part of our story—the most important part for us, come to think of it. Well, tell him, afore his grin splits his face in two!

This is told by Jing-wei her own self, of these last few days here at the Monastery of St. Edmund at Minstan, when all my life hung in a balance betwixt a Chinese future and a future here in England.

For many summers I had dreamed of escaping Tybalt's people, and somehow finding my own countryfolk again, and making for myself a better life. The dream had half come true, when I found Old Lan and she told me of a place in the south where my own folk lived. Then, it seemed that my future was all decided, and I was happy with the plan. But I reckoned without the faithful and brave heart of Jude of Doran.

Always he was good to me, even in that hour when first we met, and he stayed to talk in Tybalt's tent, and made me smile. I loved him then. And in all our dealings after, even in the times when we vexed one another, and quarrelled, I loved him still. I loved him for the way he wore no masks, made no pretence. There is no boastful-ness in him, and in his gentleness and courtesy he is mindful of what I think and feel, and holds my happiness equal to his own. He is true in all his ways, and speaks only that which lies within his heart. There is gentle strength in him, and great courage, though he sees this not himself. It was to help him find that courage that I went with him to the dragon's lair, so he would do the thing that alone could give him peace. He thought I went because I was bewitched; and mayhap I was, but not by Lan. I was bewitched by him—by the goodness in his heart.

And I came to know well his heart, through all that we endured together. And the more I knew, the more I admired. But I never knew his feelings for me, for of those he never spoke. I thought he felt, in some hidden corner of his soul, that I was an alien, apart and separate from his world. He seemed so bent on taking me to find my own people that I believed it was all he wanted for me. I thought that, though he liked me well enough, he longed for me to be safe among my own kin, so he would be free of the worry of me, free to go and take up his own life again. So when Chen came, my heart was torn in two.

Chen offered me all that I had hoped for, these long years: he offered me a home in my own land, among people like myself. He offered me, as well, honour and acclaim, and riches, and a beautiful and easy life. He offered me everything, but the freedom to be myself. He wanted my feet broken and bound again. In all else he loved me well—but in the matter of my feet, he would have enslaved my soul.

So I bided my time, not knowing what to do. And then, in this present hour, I was in the herb garden weeding among the plants, my heart forlorn, when Jude came. Running as if his life was in peril, he was, falling over the bushes in his eagerness; and he took my hands in both of his and asked me—all shining-eyed and scarlet-cheeked and with his tongue stammering—if I would be his wife.

It was so sudden I could say nought at first, and he took my silence for refusal, and began to walk away, slow and with his shoulders bowed. I called him back, and ran to him, and did what I had longed to do all summer—I put my arms around his neck and kissed his face, and told him of my love, and we both embraced, standing there among the herbs, laughing and crying as if we were half crazed. He would have run straight back to tell you, Brother Benedict, but I said I wanted that pleasure for myself. And I wanted Jude to know, too, why I love him, and have loved him long.

So that is my tale, its ending and its new beginning.

Oh Benedict, I'm almost out of my mind for joy! My heart's going like a smithy's hammer, and won't calm down! I don't know how I'll ever gather back my wits enough to finish telling you this history.

Jing-wei is meeting Chen now, to tell him of her decision. I feel sad for him, for I know that in his way he loves her. I still don't know why I'm so blessed. I'm sure I'm not all those things she says I am. Still, I'll not quarrel with her—'twould not be a good omen this early in our betrothal. Now, where were we in our narrative? I remember: the day we killed the dragon.

For the rest of that day, I slept. That night we ate sea-food again, and at dawn the next day left the cove, leaning on one another. Miraculously, we found our donkey not far from where we had abandoned it. It seemed well enough, though I could feel its ribs beneath my hands, and its hide was stiff with dust or ash. Jing-wei rode and I stumbled alongside, my hand on the donkey's neck to guide me. When the sun was fully up, and hot, Jing-wei bathed my face again with the oil, taking care about my eyes. My skin was blistering but my eyelids began to return to their normal size, and for moments I could separate the lids and glimpse the light. In the hottest part of the day we rested, reclining in the shade of a wall in a ruined village. By that evening, to my huge relief, I could open my eyes properly.

For several days we travelled, going south in search of the town where Jing-wei's countryfolk lived. We left the scorched lands and found ourselves in peaceful countryside with villages where church bells tolled, and sheep and oxen grazed the fields shorn of their rye and wheat. Jing-wei gleaned some of the stalks of grain from the edges that were left, and wove me a passable hat to shelter my burned face from the sun. I must have looked odd, for people stared as they passed us on the roads. I suppose Jing-wei looked strange to them, too, with her almond eyes and brown skin. Though curious, people were friendly, and every night we were offered a barn to sleep in, or the floor by a cosy hearth. Perchance they felt sorry for us, me with my burned face and hands, for we were fed well, too. Even our donkey got fed well, and slept in stalls with ample hay, and each day got a brushing with a bunch of twigs.

Life began to seem incredibly, wondrously normal. I realised how long I had lived in fear, how stretched my nerves had been, how close my wits to being lost. There was a huge joy in me, despite the pain of my burns, and I felt I had woken up from a dreadful dream. The world, it seemed, had woken up. People were cheerful, and travellers had lost that haunted look. There were fewer burned villages here in the south, and those we passed were being rebuilt. There was hope in the air, brought with the cool and the autumn winds. And another thing came with summer's end: the rumour that the dragon was slain.

The first time we heard it was while we stayed in the village of Trute, about ten miles north of here. We were staying with a farmer and his wife, eating at their rough trestle table with their five daughters, when one of the maids said she'd heard a marvellous thing that day. "That dragon that plagued the northern lands," she said, "is dead. Killed by a soldier with a single blow."

"There never was a dragon, Tilly, so don't talk nonsense," said her father. "It was the plague again, fallin' in fire from the skies, what killed folks and burned their crops and villages."

"It were a dragon, father!" cried Tilly, red-faced with excitement. "The juggler who told us was told by a tinker, who mended pots for a miller's wife whose husband heard it from a smith who shod the knight's horse! The knight was on his way home from the dragon's cove. St. Alfric's Cove it was, he said, and described how he'd killed the beast with a single blow. So mighty was that blow that the world shook, and the cliff fell down into the sea. The soldier left his sword in the pile of stones, to prove it, and the tip of the dragon's tail he laid nearby, to show what was buried there. He's ridden all up and down the lands, telling folks he's killed the beast and there's no need to go a-fearing any longer."

"I wasn't a-fearing, to start with," growled her father. "Leastwise, not a-fearing 'bout anything except bein' browbeaten by a bunch of frenzied women in me own house."

Jing-wei glanced at me, and we grinned at one another over our thick chunks of oatmeal bread. I had half a mind to tell them the truth, but knew I'd be laughed to scorn.

The next day we journeyed on, asking at all the villages if they knew of a town where Chinese people lived. They had never heard the word *Chinese*, and they stared wonderingly at Jing-wei and shook their heads. Jing-wei began to be troubled, thinking we would never find her own people, or maybe that they had gone back to China. Truth to tell, I didn't mind if they had gone. I was enjoying this time in Jing-wei's company, walking the country lanes and wandering across fields being sown with wheat and rye, and talking with the lads who were chasing off the crows. Several times we got lost, cutting across those open fields, for I tried to avoid the roads that ran through woods and places that might have hid thieves. Sometimes we met up with other travellers, and our way was made merry with songs and stories. Again and again we heard how the dragon was killed: sometimes by the king's army; sometimes by a lone and brave knight; sometimes by a hoard of angels who sang a heavenly note and made the cliff fall down upon the beast; sometimes by a beauteous maid using enchantment.

And so we came, eventually, to Minstan, and your Monastery of St. Edmund. Well do I remember that first night in your guest house, lying on a bed of soft straw with clean sheets, having eaten at a proper table with silver spoons, fine basins, and a polished saltcellar worth more than everything my father ever owned. I was not accustomed to so many people, for there were thirty or more of us lined up in our beds along the walls. We were a motley lot, pilgrims and traders, craftsmen and messengers; and the noise, even in the middle of the night, was horrendous. There was praying going on, and children howling, and there was snoring, and farting, and . . . Well, you don't need to know it all. Just be thankful for your quiet cell, and being disturbed only by bells summoning you to prayers.

I was walking in the cloisters the next morning, admiring the porches with their carven columns and vaulted ceilings, and looking out at the herb garden in the courtyard, thinking how peaceful it was, when I first met your Abbot. We got talking, and he asked me where I was from and where I was bound, and why. And for some reason—the kindliness of him, mayhap—I told him all. And the rest you know.

Tomorrow I'll be leaving here, to take up my work at the Abbot's goose farm. 'Tis not far from here, so I hope you'll be able to come and visit us often. I would like to see you again, Benedict, for you are as a brother to me and I hold you in much affection. I thank you with all my heart, for writing out so well this tale of mine.

And it is good to think that I shall have a hand in making more books, even if I do just keep you copiers in quills. Mayhap I'll go to the Abbot's school in my spare time, and Jing-wei can teach me to read and write. Then I won't have to bother you again if I do anything heroic on the goose farm, that needs to be made into a book. Don't smile, Benedict; we never know what the fates have in store for us, and even goose farming may have its dangerous moments.

Talking of fate, I'd like to see Old Lan again sometime, and kiss her wise old cheek. I hope one day to find Tybalt again, too, and tell him what happened to his son and where he lies. I'd like Tybalt to see Jing-wei as she is now, free and praiseworthy and strong. But I suppose she always was those things, and what is changed in her is but the size of her shoes, and the measure of her strength.

As for myself . . .

I am put in mind of that last night at home in Doran, when I was sorely disgruntled, and thought that fate was against me. I said, if I remember aright, that mayhap some saint in heaven looked down that night, and decided to stir up my pot. Well, doubtless he did, and stirred with all his might; but the mixture's fine to me.

And so my tale is done.

AUThOR'S NOTE

In Jude's time, in 1356, monks were still copying out books by hand. These manuscripts were priceless, some beautifully illustrated, the first letters of chapters and paragraphs wonderfully designed. The books were made of vellum or parchment, created from the skins of sheep or calves. The skins were cleaned, scraped on both sides, then rubbed smooth with powdered pumice. Because books were so valuable, reading was taught only to the wealthy, and teachers were usually monks. Any knowledge not taught by the Church—such as Lan's—was looked upon with suspicion.

At that time paper was rare in England, though in China paper had already been widely used for centuries, along with wooden blocks and moveable clay type for printing. In the eighth century Chinese methods of making paper had spread to Arab countries, and by the twelfth century the craft of papermaking was established also in Spain and Italy. However, in England paper was seen as a product of Moslem culture and was therefore disapproved of.

But the way of making books was to change: in Germany, in about 1450, a printing press was invented. Soon afterwards a wealthy English merchant visited Germany, and, being interested in literature, he learned the new way of producing books. His name was William Caxton. In 1476, one hundred and twenty years after Jude went to work on the Abbot's goose farm, William Caxton set up the first printing press in England. Paper, the ideal material to print on, was at first imported; but this new art, too, was learned, and soon paper was manufactured all over England.

With the invention of the printing press, history was forever changed. The painstaking work of monks slowly copying books by hand, using animal skins, feather quills, and ink, was rendered unnecessary. Books were printed in English instead of in Latin, the old language of the Church. For the first time even ordinary people, like Jude, had access to books—and to knowledge.

Printing presses were not the only invention slow to come to England. About Jude's time gunpowder was only beginning to be used, though, as Lan had predicted, the time would come when it would be a major weapon on every battlefield. And in England kites, as flying machines, were still unknown. Both kites and gunpowder had already been used in China for centuries. Only someone like Jing-wei, who had experience of both, would have been able to help Jude kill the dragon the way it was slain in this story.

Jing-wei's story of her childhood spent in the great and prosperous city of Hangchow, in China, is based on historical fact. The famous medieval traveller and author Marco Polo told of the Chinese city of Hangchow, describing it as one of the finest and noblest cities in the world. Also from history is the Chinese custom of foot binding. This custom lasted from the tenth century until 1911, when foot binding was abolished. There are still some elderly Chinese women today whose feet are bound.

Many of the medieval terms and sayings in this book—for example, "Godspeed," "plight my word," "God's nails and blood"—I gleaned from the writings of Geoffrey Chaucer, a writer from Jude's time. While Jude's English would have been very different from our own, he would have used these expressions.

As for dragons: There are dragons recorded in the legends, stories, and artwork of many nations, throughout many centuries. Were all those dragons merely figments of the imaginations of storytellers and artists? Or did such animals really exist?

I like to think they did.

Sherryl Jordan
May 2000—The Chinese Year of the Dragon

DATE DUE
